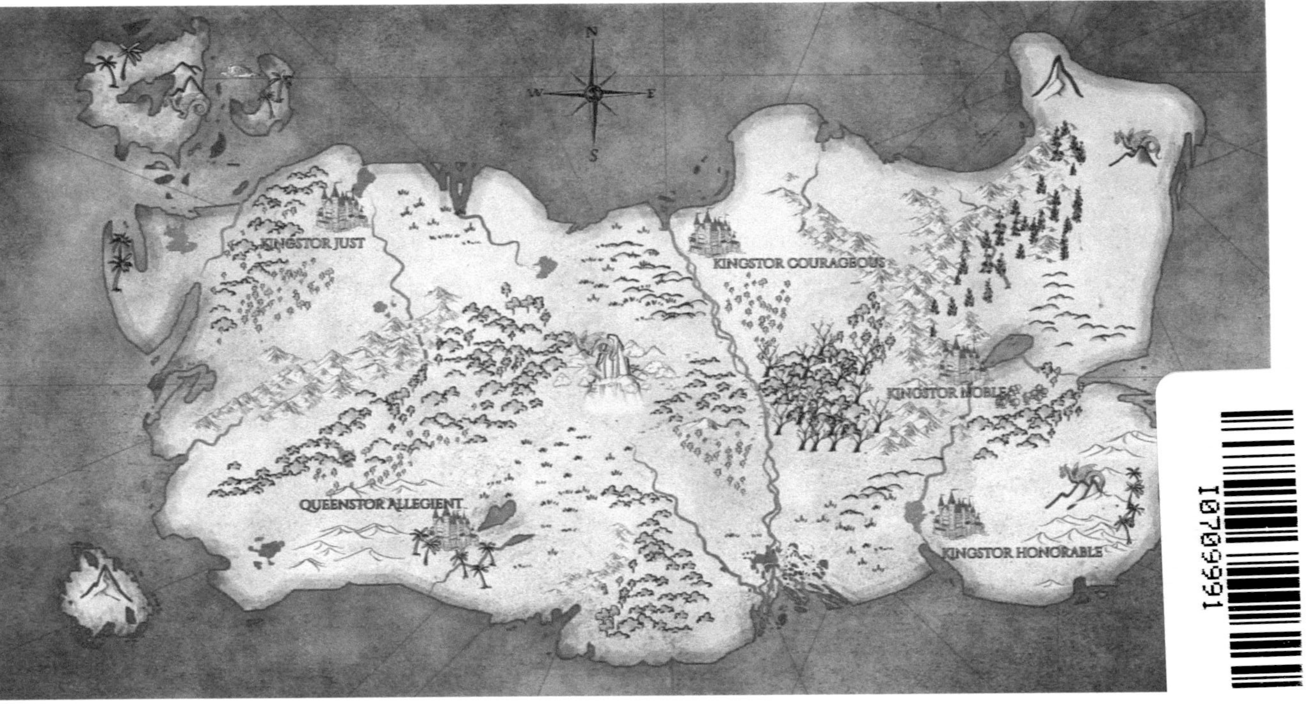

I0709991
KINGSTOR JUST
KINGSTOR COURAGEOUS
KINGSTOR NOBLE
KINGSTOR HONORABLE
QUEENSTOR ALLEGIENT

THE SHADOW OF AVONOA

THE SHADOW OF AVONOA

HRB COLLOTZI

AVONOA SERIES BOOK TWO

ISBN: 978-1-962628-12-9
Library of Congress Control Number: 2015913067
Published by HRB Collotzi
Rosemount, Minnesota

www.avonoa.com

This book is dedicated to my kids, Josh, Ashley, and
Ryan!
May you always live like the centaurs who are named after
you!
Be mindful of the future,
See to the present,
And never regret the past.
I love all of you with all my heart!

CONTENTS

1

AUDIENCES

"The faeries are angry, Philip," Torgon said while slumping on a plush blue cushion in a carved mahogany chair in the king's office. Although he didn't reach Philip's own height—few men did, even though Philip was only sixteen years old—Torgon seemed a tangle of spidery legs sprawled in that chair. The nineteen-year-old Royal General didn't adhere to formalities like sitting up straight when no one but the king was around.

Philip stared out the arched window watching the storm clouds of fall encroaching against the castle walls. "As if we could do anything about it," he grumbled.

"They claim Ortym was an invaluable member of the majikal community. Not to mention, the cousin of Kradik," Torgon said, perusing the recent letter they'd received from the Faerie Council. "They say his death at the hands of the dragon would never have happened if you'd allowed Kradik and Ortym to kill the dragon how they suggested."

Philip snorted. "Meager excuses if you ask me." When he heard nothing from his friend and advisor, Philip turned to inspect his face. "Don't tell me you agree with them?"

"Of course not." He shook his shaggy black hair and tossed the letter back onto Philip's gilded desk. "But excuses to what end?"

Philip turned back to the looming clouds with a sigh. "That's what I'd like to know."

"Sire," Murthur's voice came from the door. "It's time for your general audience."

"Thank you, Murthur." Philip moved aside the letters he and Torgon had been looking over to follow his servant and Royal General into the audience hall.

The two thrones in the audience hall occupied the far side of the room, opposite the great double entry doors under a muted blue canopy hemmed in silver embroidery. Stale color from the leaden sky dappled the floor through the large stained-glass windows which depicted heroic scenes from the kingdom's history. Large tapestries of finely woven material exhibiting scenes of gods and kings swathed the walls between the windows. Entering the hall through his private entrance near the thrones, Philip took his seat at the top of the dais.

Since the young king's official coronation last month, many nobles near and far had come to swear undying fealty. After the customary month of mourning, Philip had to suppress his anguish at the loss of his father, King Paudie, upon seeing only two thrones in the audience hall and so many portraits removed. His father's likeness now joined those of the past rulers of the Noble Kingdom on the wall in the Hall of Kings. In the audience hall, instead of his father's portrait hanging behind the central throne, only Philip's portrait remained.

His newly found sister, Princess Anna, would use the other throne. When she married, her husband would become the heir to the kingdom, unless Philip produced an heir. The royal artistry had yet to finish Anna's portrait to grace the wall. Other than her brief appearance at Philip's coronation, he'd seen her for only a short time since. Now she had disappeared. Yet again.

So Philip found himself wondering if she did indeed plan to help him in his duties as the ruler of this kingdom or continue to disappear and reappear every few days. Today, it seemed, he would be holding an audience for the general population by himself.

Thankfully, the one person Philip most relied upon, Torgon, his Royal General, took his usual position on the right side of Philip's throne. Although only nineteen years old, Torgon displayed the kind of wisdom his father, General Bragon, would have been proud of. Philip often took advantage of Torgon's wisdom and kindness, both in and out of audiences.

Thunder shook the windows in the hall as he entered. The near-permanent storm clouds of fall rolled over them. Although the kingdom hadn't seen but a small amount of rain so far, everyone knew the gales of fall to be treacherous. Anyone braving the falling sky had desperate reason to do so. Travelers were more common in winter, the three months previous, than in fall. Luckily, the severe weather kept general audiences short.

"Sire," Murthur said, once Philip gained his throne, "with your permission, Master Turner from Garden Farlinian."

The double doors opened at the opposite end of the room and a person resembling a farmer entered with his head down.

"Master Turner?" Philip said. "What do you require of your king?"

The older gentlemen wrung his hat in his hands into an incomprehensible form. As the man bent on one knee, Philip could see his thick white hair.

"I was chosen from among our villagers to beg the king's assistance in a dreadful wrong." The man bit his lip.

When he didn't continue, Philip urged him on. "Now is your chance to seek justice, Master Turner. Tell me who wronged you."

If it was possible, the man's head bent further forward. "The King's Guard," he all but whispered.

Philip's brow creased. "Tell me what happened." He knew the guards weren't perfect, but he couldn't believe their actions might be all that horrible. His men were specially trained to maintain order and law in the land and paid from taxes. The king charged them with being guards of the people as well as guards of himself.

"The guard has been abusing the people of my village, Sire. Taking food and drink without compensation. Berating the good men that stand up to them and…" he glanced up at the king, but shot his eyes to the floor again, "harming women and children, Sire."

Philip tried, but couldn't make eye contact with the troubled man. In the silence of the audience hall Philip could hear the snorts of indignation from a few nobles. He knew many of them would think it their right as superior citizens to do anything they chose. It seemed the King's Guard also held this esteem of themselves, probably supported by the nobles. In fact, this was the main reason Philip decided to begin these general audiences.

"Did you complain to their superiors about the behavior?"

"Yes, Sire." Turner lifted his head, but didn't quite meet the king's eyes. "Our area is under a new lieutenant. We tried to complain to Captain Shurgar about the lieutenant and his men, but he insisted it was just a misunderstanding. Nothing has changed for weeks, Sire."

"So Captain Shurgar is allowing the lieutenant's behavior to continue?"

"Yes, Sire."

Philip turned to Torgon. "Which general is over the area?"

"I believe it's General Riddig, Sire."

"Ah," Philip answered. He knew General Riddig. Riddig didn't take complaints from commoners. He was an old, fat general and extremely set in his ways. He had many friends among the generals and nobles. As a child Philip had always been afraid of him for seemingly no reason. Now, as a king, the man was a thorn in Philip's ankle he was afraid to remove. His father had tried to insist the old man listen to complaints from villagers, but allowed him to resume his distance when it only made things worse. Philip warned Torgon to be very careful whom he appointed as Riddig's men for the area.

Philip turned his attention back to Turner. "Is it the lieutenant making things difficult or just his men?" he asked the man.

"The men weren't difficult before Murzod was appointed, Sire," Turner answered. "But since his arrival, he's put strange ideas in their heads."

When Murzod's name came up, Philip and Torgon shared a knowing glance that Turner didn't notice. Philip nodded when the man finished. "I understand your difficulty. General Torgon will have Lieutenant Murzod reassigned. If the men give your village any more trouble, send word to the castle to Royal General Torgon and we'll investigate whether a change in captain is necessary as well. General Torgon will give you Lieutenant Murzod's reassignment papers before you leave."

Master Turner bowed deeply on one knee. "Thank you, Your Majesty. May Shurka smile on you."

As the man left the audience hall, Philip turned back to Torgon. In a low voice, he said, "Station Murzod here at the castle to keep him out of trouble. We'll figure out what to do with him later."

Murthur began to announce the next person in line for a general audience. But before he could finish, the doors burst open again. Two guards practically dragged a man—half-ragged and the rest drenched—in from the torrent outside. The pale, bone-thin man shook, although from the look on his face it was hard to tell whether from cold or fright.

One guard deposited the man on the floor and knelt to salute his king. "Sire, I apologize for the interruption. This man claimed urgency."

Philip was glad to see the other guard stay with the afflicted man instead of standing on ceremony. "No need to apologize," Philip said, rising from his throne. He came down from the dais to stoop over the withering man. "What's happened?" he asked. "Who are you?"

The man turned his widened eyes to the king. It didn't seem to bother him that King Philip looked him in the eye. After a poignant example from his sister some weeks ago, Philip had been trying to re-train himself in this habit. "My name is Roth, Sire. I bring grave news." The guard who knelt on the floor removed his own cloak to cover the drenched man. Roth struggled to still his convulsions before continuing. "We live near the forest of the faeries in the north of the kingdom along the Torthoth Mountains. The faeries sent word of a black creature attacking villages on the other side of the mountains. It hunts at night killing men, women, children and livestock. But it only kills them; it doesn't eat anything or even carry it away. It can wipe out an entire village in a single night. No one can stop it."

"That's in the Courageous Kingdom," Torgon said from Philip's side.

"Has word gone to King Torodov?" Philip asked Roth.

He nodded his head with more vigor, blinking his eyes. "Yes, but the faeries insisted we warn you."

"Why?" Philip asked, but he had a feeling he knew the answer.

"They say," Roth whispered, licking his lips, "it moves toward Kingstor Noble—toward you, not the Courageous Kingdom. They say," he gasped for breath, "it's the black dragon seeking revenge."

———

As if Philip's day couldn't get any worse, he still had one last meeting to dread. The rest of the general audience went as usual. Philip saw to the well-being of the man Roth, then settled disputes over debts and petty crimes from the rest of the villagers. In the evening before last meal, duty forced him to the private council chamber.

In this chamber he met with dignitaries for many different reasons. Originally it was built as a place to sign treaties or see to other matters of state, but there had been no reason to sign treaties for many centuries. They sat around a large round table so that no one had an advantage, as the king at the head of a table might have. On the walls hung maps of the kingdoms of Avonoa and the entire land. The maps included the lands of the centaurs, faeries and even the different dragon rucks, although these areas weren't as detailed as the human portions. At the top of the high walls hung all of the flags from the Five Kingdoms of Avonoa. To keep out any intruders or interruptions this room had been designed with no windows. A single door at the front and a door at the back led into different halls and provided the only entries—and escapes.

Philip stood when the northernmost door opened. Murthur stood behind Philip, next to the fireplace in the wall. Torgon also stood from his chair at the right of his king. The guards outside the door allowed two faeries into the room. Philip noticed they wore their traditional cloaks, but they were lighter than the ones he had seen them wear in the winter and dry despite the rain. They also wore thin leather bindings on their feet and black face coverings halfway up the cowl of their cloaks. Philip knew their hands were also gloved, but these were tucked into the cloaks' front folds.

The faeries bowed low and Philip returned a nod. "Welcome to the Noble Kingdom." Even though most faeries' slight builds only came up to Philip's nose, he couldn't shake the devious feeling he got from any faerie. Even with the faeries facing the firelight, Philip could only see the flickering reflection in their eyes within the cloaked cowls and nothing more.

"Thank you for seeing us, King Philip." The hems of the cloak on the faerie who addressed him had an intricate black pattern. Philip was glad to see he would be able to tell these faeries apart. His voice was low enough to recognize as male, but smooth enough to mistake for kind. "I am Qialla," the faerie said with another bow, "from the Faerie Council. I believe you know Kradik," he said with a wave of his hand to his companion.

The second faerie dipped his head, but said nothing.

"Yes," Philip answered. "I'm sorry for the loss of your apprentice and cousin."

"This is what we've come to discuss," Qialla said approaching the table, but he didn't sit.

Philip remembered the faerie traditions his ambassador had reviewed with him before the meeting. He swept his hand palm down over the surface of the table as if to wipe it off. It was a movement a king certainly would never do among humans, but it was required by a visiting faerie before they would sit, as if to prove the cleanliness of their environment. But the faeries continued to stand.

Irritated, Philip stilled the toe tapping inside his boot. "Please be seated, my friends." He swiped his hand over the table again.

"Thank you," Qialla said, "but are you sure we won't be interrupted by Princess Anna?"

"I haven't seen her for three days," Philip said, "but it would be within her rights to join us."

Qialla stood up straighter. "We will not discuss these things in front of the woman."

Philip's brow creased. Despite himself he leaned toward them. "Why is that? Has she done something to offend you?" Perhaps they could define why Philip constantly felt unease around her. "Is she not who she says she is?"

"She is exactly who she claims to be," Qialla answered with a sharp tone. "This is precisely why we won't trust her with any of our plans or information. More I cannot tell you."

"Very well," Philip nodded. "Murthur," he said over his shoulder, "inform the guards not to allow the princess in while we're in council."

Once this had been cleared, the faeries finally took their seats across from the king. Almost like a trick of the light, the delicate patterns on the back of their cloaks that were their wings lifted to their sides as they sat, instead of curving around their bodies in the chairs. "You received the letter from the Faerie Council, I assume?" Qialla asked.

"I did," Philip answered, "although I'm not sure what the council is asking me to do. There is no way for me to track a dragon. I have declared that dragons be killed on sight, but I'm unsure of how to respond with anything more."

"Let me explain." From within his cloak Qialla produced both of his gloved hands in fists. "The council has recently been made aware of a weakness of the dragons'. We're working on a way to exploit it." He opened his left fist to display a bulbous red mushroom, the rounded bottom sitting in his palm and snaking tentacles with orange tips reaching up, making it look like fire frozen in time. "Do you know the flarote plant?"

Philip nodded, but Torgon answered. "It has medicinal properties. I thought it was used to heal animals, not harm them."

"Every substance in the world," Qialla said, "has the ability to harm or heal—the difference is in how it is broken down, what it's mingled with and the amount consumed.

"In this situation, we have learned through secret sources that if a dragon eats too many of these healing plants, it will kill him. This," he opened his right hand to reveal a white powder, "is what the council proposes the Noble Kingdom help us research and eventually put into use."

Philip stared at the substance. "This is what you used on the black dragon just two months ago, isn't it?"

He directed his question to Kradik, who simply nodded in return.

"This powder can render a dragon unconscious," Qialla said. "But it is only temporary, it's not deadly and it must be used in close proximity. We propose researching a way to concentrate it, in hopes it will be fatal."

Philip glanced at Torgon, who said, "You realize who we would need to test this on?"

"If you're afraid," Qialla sneered, "we will be here to assist you the entire way."

When Torgon's mouth opened to retort, Philip put a reassuring hand on his general's arm. "Our men will be able to fulfill whatever role is asked of them, but we need to understand fully what that will entail."

Qialla replaced both gloved fists in his cloak. "The Great Northern Mountain is rich with flarote year round. We need to pass through your kingdom in order to obtain it. Your citizens, as well as ours, will gather any dragon ash they can find. And we require you to supply the men for the hard labor to gather and grind large amounts of flarote."

"Will it be dangerous work?" Philip asked.

"No," Qialla answered, "just labor intensive. The faeries, I'm sure you're aware, aren't many. We have few resources of men to fuel the effort."

Philip nodded, but Torgon spoke from his side. "What do you mean when you say you need us to 'put it into use'?"

Philip tried to see into Qialla's dark cowl as he answered. "You will need more than a few men to hunt dragons. The council won't be pleased with anything less than death for the black demon dragon and any others who get in our way. We are ready to completely align ourselves to the humans in a war against these flying monsters."

Philip was somewhat taken aback. "You want me to declare war on the black dragon?" He glanced at Torgon for support. "I have no intention of attacking it directly, or the other dragons. That would be extremely perilous to all humans."

Kradik finally spoke, slowly standing from his chair. "'Perilous'" he emphasized the word, "was you insisting on capturing a dragon. 'Perilous' was you insisting on using it as a trophy. And what would be most 'perilous' is you choosing to allow such a threat to every gentle species in all of Avonoa to continue to exist."

Qialla calmed him with a single raised hand. After Kradik resumed his seat, Qialla spoke again. "Consider this, King Philip. The creature attacked a faerie village as well. The faeries and the council feel that you and the humans are directly responsible for the black dragon's behavior. If you choose not to help us in our efforts to abate the threat of these monsters, then the Faerie Council has instructed me to inform you that the Noble Kingdom will be our destination after we've dealt with the dragons."

2

DEMANDS

"I was trapped like a bird with a broken wing in a deep, dark hole." Hiro stared in turn into each glowing eye of the hatchlings surrounding him. None of them blinked at the pure black dragon. "They took turns beating me." A little gray hatchling named Tutto gave a small gasp. "For weeks the humans allowed a procession of abusers to assail me. I was starved, frozen and bloodied day and night." A few tiny maws hung open at his words.

Although Hiro had been forbidden to tell the hatchlings anything of the faeries' involvement in his capture and the torture they inflicted, he still managed to express the horror of being face-to-face with the volatile humans. The only problem with his story was…

"How did you escape, Hiro?" The question came from the one dragon, much too old for this group, sitting in the back. Prakyndar, or Prak as everyone called him, was a small brown dragon with light brown spikes running down both sides of his spine from crown to tail. His name meant "sharp" and he was definitely smart. But everyone, other than his own sires, called him Prak, not for his legerity, but because he was more like a thorn under their scales. His name rang true to Hiro when he asked the one question Hiro had difficulty answering.

"Well," Hiro started, gave a tiny roll to his shoulder while he stopped to think. He and Rakgar agreed that the young dragons shouldn't be told of Princess Anna helping Hiro escape his chains. The humans, with the possible exception of the woman, didn't know of the dragons' intelligence. They felt as if telling the hatchlings would only raise their hopes of having a human help them or be kind to them in some way—which, of course, grown dragons knew to be impossible. Besides, he still felt like he owed the woman a debt and he hated himself for it. The problem was, his tale took on a different ending almost every time he told it.

"He tore at the chains with his own claws!" an animated voice exclaimed behind him. Hiro turned to see Tog, his best friend, crouching behind them. Tog was a gray dragon roughly Hiro's size, but Tog had several horns on the back of his head while Hiro only had two. Tog also had short ridges running the length of his spine and Hiro had none.

Hiro knew he must have been more excited about his own story than he realized in order to let another dragon sneak up on him. Hiro turned back to the hatchlings whose faces now lit with excitement. "Which is how I lost this." He held up his left front claw and waggled the stump where a fourth talon should've been.

At this, all the little dragons gasped and let out a raucous cheer. "Yay!"

"He escaped!" one screamed.

"Death to humans!" another roared.

"Our hero!" Tutto called over the din.

As they began to chant "Hiro! Hiro! Hiro!" he turned to hunt for the usual grin on Tog's face when the story ended. But this time his friend looked him sternly in the eye.

"I need to see you back in your cave," he told Hiro while the hatchlings roared and spit little bursts of fire.

Hiro nodded to his friend. "Alright!" he called to the youngsters. "Head to the feeding grounds. Your parents will meet you there."

"Hiro!" Prak ran up to the black dragon before Hiro and Tog had a moment to speak. The young dragon had always liked Hiro, but when he'd come back from the surface and gained the name of Hiro, Prak took it upon himself to be Hiro's personal shadow. "I'm taking the Krusible tomorrow. Will you come and await me, Hiro? I'm sure I'll pass it. Milah and Mitashio are usually pretty nice to me. Are you coming to the feeding grounds too, Hiro? Can we fly together?"

"No, but…" Hiro tried to speak, but Prak cut him off.

"Where are you going?" Prak rattled on in a high, nasal voice. "Have you eaten already? Are you going somewhere with Priya? Can I come, too?"

"No!" Tog and Hiro roared together.

Hiro didn't meant to be so brusque with the younger dragon, but Tog had a deadly look in his eye. One Hiro hadn't seen for a long time.

"I'll see you tomorrow morning at the Krusible, Prak." Hiro and Tog pushed past the younger dragon toward the entrance of the cave. "What's wrong?" Hiro finally asked his gray friend in a low voice.

"We have a problem." Tog turned his back to follow the hatchlings out of the cave.

Hiro had taught the hatchlings in Rakgar's lair that day because it was the safest place for them to meet. With the storm clouds of fall gathering everywhere, outside any lair wasn't very safe for flying. Many of them couldn't even fly yet. They would crawl to the feeding grounds and their dames and dans would carry them back to their homes in the floating mountains of the Rock Clouds where the dragon ruck lived. Hiro had convinced Rakgar of the necessity to begin teaching the youngsters of the dangers of humans much earlier, hoping to avoid anything happening to them like what had happened to Hiro only weeks previous.

Hiro followed his friend, but questioned him again to see what might be bothering him. "Don't tell me it's Surneen," he said with a mischievous grin.

Surneen was the dame Tog had kept both of his toggling eyes on since they were fledglings. Hiro knew Tog harbored a hard spot in his heart for her.

Tog stopped. "Sur….What?" he asked with a creased brow.

Hiro just rolled his eyes. "You know what I'm talking about."

"Hiro," Tog grabbed Hiro's front leg to stop him from moving, focusing one dangerous eye on his friend. "This is much more serious than that." He let go and bolted into the sky.

More serious than your heart breaking for a dame? Hiro thought, jumping after his friend. *What's more serious than that?*

The sky hung heavy with thick, dark clouds, yet it hadn't started raining. Three months of rain wasn't usually desirable to a dragon, but these rains melted away any snow from winter, warmed the ground and brought spring buds soon thereafter. As long as dragons could fly above or around the bad storms, they tolerated the season well.

The clouds just began to shed wet drops when Hiro and Tog landed on the edge of his cave. Dashing inside to avoid the torrent, Hiro almost started questioning Tog again when a movement near the wall caught his eye. His lair wasn't very large; it only had space enough for a family of three, actually. He lived there all his life with his parents until they died. Now their lair was his own, so no one else should have been there.

Searching out the movement, Hiro saw something he had hoped never to see again. He froze. His breath stopped. Princess Anna, with her golden hair cascading over her shoulders, pushed off the wall to stare wide-eyed at the two dragons. She wore a deep purple dress with gold trim on the wrists and hem that matched her hair. Although the gown must have been made of rich material, it looked like she had crawled through muddy rose bushes in it.

Hiro jerked his head back to Tog with a crease seared above his eyes. His own pulse pounded in his ears. What could his friend possibly mean by bringing a human here? Especially this human! Hiro's lips parted, but he couldn't bring himself to question his friend. Had Tog spoken to her? Before he could think or do anything, Tog moved in front of him. Placing his nose in front of Hiro's, he breathed a memory into Hiro's face. Immediately, Hiro's vision was superimposed by Tog's memory.

He recognized the terrain of the surface world at once. It was the forest just beyond the Rock Clouds to the east. Another sight he had hoped never to see again. Piles of snow lay scattered around the muddy forest floor and gray clouds moved to cover the bare trees overhead. In front of him, Anna stepped out from behind a thick clump of trees.

Hiro knew Tog was aware of her identity because Tog had seen her in Hiro's own memories of his capture. Now in Tog's memory, Hiro crawled toward her, but she stood her ground. The human shivered from fear. Or it might have been the cold. She had no coverings on her feet or even a cloak to keep the chill out. Hiro circled her in the memory as Tog must have, brushing her skirts with his claw. He sniffed her arm and shoved her shoulder with his nose. Hiro recalled her scent with perfect clarity. Delicate and mellow, with a hint of resinous alkaline. He crept behind her. She shuddered when the dragon sniffed her hair.

When the viewpoint of the memory slithered around to face her again, she raised a hand to the gem-splattered gold trinket around her neck. With a swift yank, she pulled it off. Casting her eyes down, she offered it in a shaking hand to the dragon in front of her.

Hiro saw Tog's claw reach out for the offering. He knew Tog hoped to take the necklace and hence be allowed to leave without harming the woman, according to human belief. But just before he could retrieve the shiny offering, Anna jerked it out of his reach. With all traces of cold and fear gone, she looked deep into the dragon's face. "Take me to your hero," she demanded.

Hiro blinked back into his own body in his cave. Tog stared back with boiling anger in his eyes. Tog opened his mouth before Hiro could stop him. "Have you ever....?"

Hiro closed his eyes. "Not until this moment."

"I knew it!" Anna yelled with a smile. "I knew you could talk!"

Tog roared and turned on her with an upraised claw, but Hiro slipped between them.

"What are you doing?!" Tog yelled at him.

"Don't be a fool," Hiro growled back, although he kept his voice lower. "You can't kill her."

"What?!" the woman asked from behind him. They ignored her.

"Then what do you propose we do about it?" Tog brought his voice down along with his claw. "You know the law."

Hiro stared into his friend's eye. "I'm not going to tell anyone. Are you?"

Tog grumbled and turned to face the wall, flopping down on the ground. Hiro knew Tog hated breaking any rules, which Hiro, as Dak (as he had been called previously), had done on countless occasions in his past life. His friend always needed to be appeased or justified in some way in order not to run and tell all the other dragons of Dak's misdeeds.

"She's a princess," Hiro continued. "She'll be missed, if not worse!"

"What do you mean, 'kill' me?" Anna asked again, attempting to push past Hiro's back leg.

With narrowed eyes, Hiro faced her. "It's the law of the dragons that any human who hears a dragon speak must be killed."

Anna's face paled. "But I…"

"You tricked me," Tog blurted over his shoulder. "That's what you did."

"I'm sorry," she called to him, then locked eyes with Hiro. "I had to."

"How did she know your name?" Tog asked the wall.

Hiro cocked his head to one side. "Yes, how did you know my name?"

"I guessed," she shrugged. "I assumed the dragon that rescued another dragon would be called a great hero."

Hiro couldn't help the grin spreading across his face. "You tricked him," he said with a chuckle.

"It's not funny!" Tog gnarred over his tail at them.

Anna stepped around Hiro to approach the gray dragon. "I apologize…er…" She looked to Hiro for help.

"Tog," he informed her.

"…Tog," she continued. "I wouldn't have—"

"Wait!" Hiro threw a claw out to interrupt the human. "Tog," he snapped his neck around to his friend, "where's Priya?"

Anna watched with interest, but kept silent. Tog shrugged, "She disappeared."

"Again?" Hiro growled.

Tog rested his head on his claws. "She disappears all the time. She's a grown dame. She can handle herself."

"You're on her contingent," Hiro crouched in attack posture. "You're supposed to keep her safe."

Tog must have heard the threat in Hiro's voice because he turned his head and lifted slightly from the ground on all fours. "Don't blame me, Hiro Tekla," Tog postured in defense. "You have no right."

"I have every right!"

"No!" Tog bellowed back. "Only Rakgar has the right to find fault in my actions! I answer to him! You would only have the right to assign me blame if you would cough up your heart for her!"

Hiro glanced at Anna, who watched with wide eyes. "Don't be vulgar, Tog."

Tog eyed the woman and settled back to the floor. "I'm just saying that if you'd come to the surface with us, you wouldn't have to blame things like this on me. You'd see for yourself. Priya will be fine. She always is."

Hiro rolled his shoulder. "Maybe I will come in future."

Tog assumed his composure on the floor. "This doesn't answer the question of how that one—" he threw dagger eyes at the human, "—knew dragons could speak."

Hiro shifted his attention back to the little human. "You also claimed to know this when you freed me."

Anna backed away from their glares. "M-my father told me," she stammered. "It's a secret among royalty that he told me before he died. I wasn't even sure I believed it until you acted the way you did."

"Yet, you took the risk," Hiro pressed. "You risked freeing me and you risked coming here. Why?"

"I wouldn't have done something so dangerous except—I desperately need your help."

"Help?" he asked. "What help could you possibly need from us?"

"Something is attacking the humans," she said. "There have been reports of a dark creature attacking at night and killing people and animals."

"Just because you helped me in a time of great need," Hiro told her, "doesn't mean I owe you so much that I'll come whenever you call. I'm not a trained animal."

"I don't ask for myself." Anna stood up straighter. "The king thinks it's you attacking us."

Tog spun around at this, but Hiro asked with a half grin, "Me? Why would I do this?"

"Revenge," Anna said. "They say the monster moves toward Kingstor Noble, although it began its attacks in the Courageous Kingdom."

"How could anyone know this?"

"The path of destruction." Anna stepped toward Hiro. "It can kill dozens of humans in a single night. If you help me destroy whatever is attacking, you'll prove it wasn't you. Perhaps my brother will call off his decree to kill the dragons."

"What?!" Tog and Hiro said together.

Anna nodded. "He's ordered that any and all dragons be killed on sight."

"Then we'll just stay away from the Noble Kingdom," Tog said. "That should be simple enough."

"Keeping us out of harm's way at the same time," Hiro nodded. "Avonoa," he said to Anna, "is a large land with many humans. Request the aid of one of your own."

The hurt on Anna's face almost swayed Hiro's resolve. "You won't help me?"

Hiro sighed. "You saved my life and I saved Tog from killing you. My debt is repaid."

Guilt switched to shock when the human woman narrowed her eyes and lashed with her tongue. "Coward!" she yelled, "I thought dragons were brave and bold!" She continued her tirade, planting her tiny fists on her waist. Hiro glanced at Tog, who goggled with both eyes. "I thought you feared nothing! I thought a mighty dragon could swoop in and kill this creature and be done before the sun rose! Are you telling me you're afraid?" She stopped to glower into his eye.

"We fear no creature," Hiro bent his long neck down to her eye level, "especially little human princesses. Your insults won't harry me."

"Then you just don't care?" she asked, folding her arms across her chest.

He didn't answer.

"Don't you see? If this creature goes unchecked, it will destroy the land along with the dragons' food source," she said. "It will eventually affect the dragons, too."

"I'll do nothing without orders from my Rakgar," Hiro told her. He received a justified nod from Tog.

"What's a Rakgar?"

"Our leader," Tog said.

"Dragons have a leader?" she asked, momentarily distracted from her argument.

"Of course we do," Hiro said with a sigh.

"How would your leader feel if he knew you were such a coward?" she asked with a sneer.

Hiro leveled his eyes at her. "Don't try your little mind games with me, human. I can see past them because my brain is bigger than yours."

She planted her tiny fists on her hips again. "And how would you know? Do you sneeze it out occasionally and measure it?"

Before Hiro could answer, the sound of wings against the rain outside broke the silence, but only for him. Hiro shoved Anna against the wall where it angled deeper into the cave. "Someone's coming."

"How do you...?" she started, but was silenced with a glance of the dragon's eye.

"Hiro!" Prak called into the cave before landing.

"Prak," Hiro called back, stepping in front of the woman. "What are you doing flying around in a storm?"

"Something's happened! Rakgar desires your presence. I offered to come get you instead of one of the guard. Only a few of the huntresses have returned. Something awful has happened!" He said all this in one breath and for once, Hiro was glad Rakgar sent the little chatterer.

"We'll be right behind you," he said when Prak took a breath, then waited for the young dragon to get the hint.

"Alright," Prak said, turning back to the pounding rain. "If I get there before you, I'll tell Rakgar you'll be there in a moment. Be careful out here. There's a wicked downdraft just above your cave. I'll see you there."

Once he was out of sight again, Hiro faced Anna. "If you value your life, stay hidden while I'm gone," he sighed. "I'll take you back to the surface when I return."

"You'll take me back to die."

"You'll be no safer here," he said, baring his fangs. "I might get hungry."

As the two dragons left they both heard her scathing words behind them. "Are you sure you can brave the rain?" Hiro rolled his shoulder before he leapt into the clouds.

3

INTRIGUES

"I don't trust them." Philip moved his rook. He sat across from Torgon in the antechamber of the dining hall. The two friends had taken to a routine of playing chess after dinner lately. Although they both enjoyed the game and conversation, Philip rarely won.

"No one trusts faeries," Torgon said. He took one of Philip's pawns. Philip was unusually distracted tonight. "They cover their faces and use majik like we use water. Anyone would be a fool to trust them."

The faeries had eaten with the king and his general, but retired early to their chambers. At least this time they'd agreed to stay in one of the castle's guest chambers. Philip made sure it was large enough for esteemed guests, and held a commanding view of the forest and Teardrop Sea to gratify their love of nature.

"I will give them one point," Philip said, moving his rook to take Torgon's bishop. "They've given me reason to trust Anna."

"Oh?"

"They support her claim to royal blood even though they don't trust her. And what did your father always say?"

"'Who better to trust than my enemy's enemy,'" Torgon quoted.

"Precisely," Philip said. "But how can I learn to trust her if she's never around?"

"They did say she was safe. And that she would return." Torgon took a sip of wine.

"…From wherever she is." Philip gazed at the foggy window. "They won't tell us that, either."

"Check."

Philip took in the game again. His rook move availed him nothing. "I can't do anything but help them, can I?" he said, shifting his counterpart away from harm. "Anything else would mean war on two fronts."

"What?" Torgon chuckled. "A war with dragons? Do you fear they'll organize an offensive?"

"Worse." Philip's face showed no mirth. "If one dragon is attacking the people, killing dozens in a single night, what might they do if we openly retaliate with this poison?" He looked up at Torgon to see the grin slide from his face, then stared back at the chess board without seeing it. "We might have dragons running rampant all over the five kingdoms and faeries attacking us with majik everywhere else."

"Don't forget the centaurs who hate humans and would happily kill us on the spot should we run across them," Torgon said.

"Exactly."

Torgon moved one of his knights forward. "My father used to say something else quite frequently, as well." He looked Philip in the eye. "'There's always a choice'… Checkmate."

4

SURNEEN'S MEMORY

Hiro hoped to avoid going back out in the rain until tomorrow's lesson. It pounded on their scales making a clattering sound as the black and gray dragons flew back to Rakgar's lair. The downdrafts kept throwing him off course. The cold and wet reminded him of the torture-filled weeks he had lain in the snow with the humans. Seeing Anna again only made the anger worse.

When they landed in the massive lair, Hiro could see a number of other dragons there. Surneen sat poised in front of Rakgar. She was a deep, crimson color with large copper spots on her body and wings like a summer sunset after a particularly bloody kill, as her name suggested, meaning "Bloody Sunset." Her mother had been a desert dame, where most of them were a mix of yellow, orange or red— unlike the Rock Clouds, where the dames were usually blue, green, yellow or a mix of the three.

Milah and Mitashio hovered next to Rakgar. They both threw Hiro contemptuous looks when he entered. He knew they despised the fact that he avoided his punishment of practicing silence with them every day for an Avonoan year. He also knew the muddy brown dragons would be discussing the Krusible the next day. Probably begging Rakgar to force Hiro to attempt it one last time, just so they could fail him.

A few other dragons sat nearby waiting to discuss things with Rakgar. Hiro knew his leader found it difficult to trust another counselor as he had Hiro's own father, Tusten. Other dragons were there to feed their young ones from the strips of dried meat hanging in another room of the cavern.

Hiro and Tog knew Surneen and a dozen other dames had left earlier that morning to hunt for large kill. The supply of dried winter meat had begun to dwindle. Although they could last awhile longer in the Rock Clouds before replenishing the food, Rakgar decided to allow the huntresses to see how a fall hunt on the surface progressed—a typical practice when the rains started.

Surneen nodded to them as they entered. Tog didn't make it obvious, but Hiro noticed he held his head a little higher after returning the gesture. When Tog finally perceived Hiro's withering grin, he simply muttered, "Snap it."

Hiro turned his eyes to Rakgar. "Shining days, Rakgar. You summoned me?"

"Hiro," Rakgar greeted him as he approached the leader. "Surneen has just shared a most disturbing experience with us." He stretched his long neck toward

Hiro. "As it involves you, I would appreciate your opinion on the matter." He placed his nose in front of Hiro's and blew the warm breath of a memory into his face. In an instant Hiro's vision was superseded by the memory, which he assumed came from Surneen's point of view.

Three dames spread out on either side of him as he crept slowly through the Black Forest. He could tell it was the Black Forest because very little light peeked through the trees swaying at least five dragon lengths overhead. Most of the forest floor was only hard-packed dirt, but specks of light reflected from leftover snow clumps dotted the ground. Hiro couldn't smell it through someone else's memory, but he remembered the piney tang and sweet scent of morapa leaf.

The field of vision in the memory kept Hiro facing forward. He could sense Surneen's focus in that direction. Staring hard through the trees, he finally discerned a large creature beyond the thick tree trunks. A large, muscular tail brushed the ground. He guessed that more dames must be surrounding the beast from all angles. Group hunting.

He watched as three dames from different directions led the group forward. As they converged, Hiro made out the shape of a large, two-headed lizard: a scorrand, even bigger than the one he killed on his own a few months ago. It must be a male.

But something was wrong. The scorrand's tail brushed the ground again, but both heads stayed still. One of the lizard's massive heads hung at a strange angle, almost against the tree next to it. Hiro could feel anxiety and caution well up in the memory—the emotions must have been strong to transmit to him. Surneen realized the danger, but had no time to signal the others before they were attacked.

Suddenly from every direction arrows flew through the air like an overturned hornet nest accompanied by thick crossbow bolts the humans called "dragon-killers." Several dames roared in outrage.

The green and blue dame, two from the left, screeched when she was hit then instantly turned to a pile of smoldering embers. Shocked at the sight, Surneen began to tread backwards, still watching the slaughter around her.

Humans sprang from under false rocks and makeshift bushes they must have fashioned long ago. Another huntress dove from the sky to attack. A human man bearing the blue crest with a silver sword from the Noble Kingdom aimed an arrow at her. Hiro felt Surneen's glint of hope when the arrow left only a ribbon of blood on the dame's neck. But hope died as quickly as she did. Three heavy dragon-killers pinned her to a tree before she landed.

Two more dames looked like they sprouted quills of arrows and bolts before they died. A dark orange dame with streaks of silvery yellow raked her claws at four men. She might have lived if they hadn't surrounded her. They took turns stabbing into her legs and wings to immobilize her before she fell to embers.

Surneen must have realized her folly in staying. She turned to flee, but stopped face-to-face with another human man. He lifted his crossbow with a dragon-killer nocked. Hiro stared from Surneen's point of view at the large, silver-tipped bolt.

THUNK! An arrow embedded in the man's neck. Hiro saw the moment of confusion in the human's eyes. He forgot the crossbow, but pulled the trigger as he grabbed at the arrow. The would-be dragon-killer loosed into the branches well away from Surneen. Hiro turned with her in the direction the arrow had come to see a large, black centaur gallop into view.

Suddenly, more than thirty centaurs spread out through the forest, to engage the men. With guttural cries they sent their own arrows into the humans. The black centaur, as tall as Surneen, trampled a nearby attacker under his lethal hooves. Once the humans' attention shifted to their own defense, Surneen suppressed her nerves *and joined the centaurs' attack. She tore a bow and quiver from one of the men and threw him into another blue-clad human.*

Hiro watched as she culled another man from behind a stunted bush. She pounded him to the ground and stood on his chest with a raised claw to deliver the final blow. Before the blow could land, a centaur called out behind her. "Wait, Dragon!" Surneen whipped her head around at the yell. A brown centaur with long, flowing black hair and leather binding across her chest to signify her as female trotted toward them. Although he guessed that Surneen had never met her, Hiro knew the centaur to be Ashel, the leader of the warrior centaurs.

"We need to ask him some questions first," Ashel said, pointing to the groaning human.

The man under Surneen's claw shivered with fright, but managed to say, "You have power over dragons, Centaur?"

"Of course not," Ashel scoffed. "Dragons think for themselves." Surneen stepped from the man's chest as Ashel put an arrow to his face. "What majik conjured the bravery for human men to attack a group of huntresses?"

The man's eyes twitched among Ashel, the arrow and the dragon. "It was a trap," he finally murmured.

Ashel glanced up at Surneen briefly. Surneen's eyes drifted to the large scorrand, who remained unscathed through all the fighting. One of its heads was, indeed, tied to the trunk of a tree, as she feared.

"How dare you?!" Ashel's large eyes blazed. She pulled her bow to full strength.

"It was meant for the black dragon." The man shrank from the tip of her arrow. "But we were ordered to kill any dragon to approach."

Ashel relaxed her bow string. She narrowed her eyes to survey the area. "Why would the Noble Kingdom set a trap for a single dragon?"

The man sat up. No longer feeling his life was in danger, he spoke freely. "King Philip has declared war on the black demon dragon in response for the attacks on human villages." He jerked his head at the piles of dragon embers. "He offers large rewards for dragon ash, too."

Ashel kept her arrow in hand, but draped her bow across her chest while she watched the other centaurs gathering. "Did any other dragons survive?" she asked the black centaur who had saved Surneen's life.

"None that we've found, but some might've escaped into the sky," he said. Human gore still dripped from his front hooves.

Ashel placed a hand on Surneen's shoulder. "Go back to the Rock Clouds, my friend." The man sitting at her feet narrowed his eyes at the gesture. Surneen eyed him back. "Don't worry," Ashel jerked her head at the man, "I'll take care of this."

Hiro's gaze shifted when Surneen turned around to search for an opening in the trees. As she crawled away from the human and the centaurs she heard a swish. She glanced back in time to see the man slump to the ground with a gaping wound in his neck and Ashel standing over him with the bloody arrow tip in her hand.

The memory ended, but Hiro stared at Rakgar in amazement. Rakgar then stepped over and gave Tog the same memory. Since it took only moments for the receiver to experience, Tog blinked soon to show he had seen the same thing. He looked knowingly into Hiro's eyes.

Rakgar motioned to Hiro with his claw, but addressed the others dragons present. "Seeing as our Hiro has expressed the desire never to return to the surface again, I believe I'll have to ask for volunteers to investigate…"

"No," Hiro rolled his shoulder, hardly believing his own voice, "it's my responsibility."

"But if you're too afraid to be among humans again," Milah sneered, "I'm sure there are other, more courageous, dragons who can deal with it."

Hiro bared his fangs at the fiend. To call him "coward" in front of so many, he wanted to tear out Milah's forked tongue. "It's my fault. I'll handle it."

"Of course," a large gray dragon with a brown tail and wings spoke from Milah's side, "if the human king thinks it is Hiro attacking his people, it might be wiser to keep him here until they figure out who or what is really at fault."

"Rakgar," Hiro puffed out his chest, "allow me to investigate the cause and see if there is anything to be done. I owe this to myself and the ruck."

Rakgar glared at Hiro. Hiro maintained eye contact with the fearsome leader, but for a moment he thought he saw a glimmer of hatred in the larger dragon's eye. Hiro thought he must have imagined it when Rakgar finally announced, "You may go, if you desire." Milah shifted in place, but his mistrustful eyes never left Hiro. "But you must travel first to a faerie shaman."

Although it was not out of the ordinary for Rakgar to suggest a course of action, Hiro tilted his head in concern. "You know how I feel about them, Rakgar."

"Yes," he said, placing his nose in front of Hiro, "but do it, you shall." He passed Hiro a shortened memory of a journey to the faerie forest realm, showing Hiro the precise location of the faerie shaman so that Hiro would know it as well as if he had been there before.

"And I shall go with him!" Tog said from his side. His friend's nearest eye was on Hiro, but Hiro knew the other toggling eye watched for Surneen's reaction to his exclamation.

"I wouldn't go without you, my friend."

"Don't forget me!" a voice that seemed all snout called. Prak scurried forward to join the two bigger dragons. "I'll help, too. I'm very helpful in a tight spot. I can't wait to see the surface. I'll do whatever you ask. After all, you might need someone to relay messages or gather food or go for help, although I'd prefer to remain with you. All I need to do is pass the Krusible tomorrow. Which I'm positive I'll be able to do. I've had no trouble at all in my lessons. Please let me come with you."

When Prak finally stopped talking, Hiro tried to be gentle with him. "I'm sorry, Prak, but this is too urgent to wait." When the smaller dragon's face fell, he added, "Next time. I promise." Then he turned his attention to Rakgar. "We'll leave at dark."

Rakgar dipped his head. "Very well."

Hiro and Tog inclined their heads, but Tog fell a step behind as they loped from the cave. Just before they flew back into the rain, Hiro heard him mutter, "I'll meet you back at your cave." Without another word, his best friend raced past him and flew out. He shrugged off his friend's behavior, knowing who waited in his cave.

Luckily, the rain had eased during their discourse, but it still beat a steady patter on Hiro's back as he watched Tog disappear into the trees on the Inner Mountain. He turned his own course toward his lair and a few minutes later landed on the lip of the cave. Princess Anna poked her head around a slight curve in the rock, but Hiro said nothing. He tromped to the far wall where he usually slept and curled up on the floor.

"What happened?" she asked, but was greeted by silence. She gazed around the cave a moment then tapped her foot. "I'm not accustomed to being ignored," she almost growled at him.

"Perhaps you'd like to discuss it with Rakgar," he snarled back.

"Perhaps I should. There must be a more reasonable creature in this ruck somewhere."

He chuckled. "Rakgar would rip you to shreds before a single word passed your lips."

The bold human came to stand in front of him. "Then tell me what happened," she said with her small fists planted on her hips.

Hiro sighed. "A group of humans killed a number of huntresses." Anna's face blanched. "They set a trap for me, but killed the dames instead. I'm forced to intervene."

"So you're going to help?"

"I'm going to investigate," he clarified, wrapping his claws over his head, trying to escape the inevitable.

"When do we leave?" she asked, coming closer.

"We have to wait for dark," he said into his claws. "Then I'll fly you straight home. You can make it from the pass, I believe?"

"Look at me, you snake!" she yelled. Hiro slowly lifted his head to glare at her through narrowed eyes. "You'll take me with you or I'll tell everyone I know that you spoke to me."

"This is how you repay a kindness?" He put his head back down. "I should expect as much from a human."

She stamped her tiny foot on the rock. "I'm going with you."

"Perhaps I'll let Tog kill you after all."

"And just make things worse for you with the king."

He looked up to glare at her again, but this time she clasped her hands together in front her chest. "Please," she said, "these are my people. I need to at least learn how to protect them."

Hiro shook his head, rolled his shoulder, sat in silence for a moment, then rolled his shoulder again. "We're traveling to a faerie shaman first," he conceded. "You can learn what you need to know there, then I'll take you home."

She knelt in front of him and placed her hand on his claw. "Thank you."

Before he could say anything else, the sound of beating rain on wings outside made Hiro's ears prick. He scarcely had time to face the entrance, and none to hide the human, before Tog landed to greet them.

"Welcome back," Hiro breathed again. "Feeling better?" Tog bobbed his head. Then Hiro noticed his limp. "What's wrong with your foot?"

"Nothing," he answered, warily eyeing the human.

She waved her hands in the air. "Pardon my rudeness for not giving you some privacy."

"Never mind." He lifted his top lip at her, but all the same he moved to the opposite side of the cave. Hiro followed him.

Still only a dragon's length from the woman, they turned their backs on her. "What is it?" Hiro asked again in a lower voice. Tog held up his claw, opening it to reveal a faceted gray teardrop-shaped gem. A dragon's heart. Tog's heart.

Hiro's eyes widened. "Who?" he whispered.

Tog rolled one eye at him. "Who else?" But when Hiro didn't put it together, he whispered, "Surneen."

Hiro nodded. "Of course. But how did it happen?"

"I don't know." Tog shrugged. "It struck me that she might have died today. Then I realized I would be leaving on a dangerous quest and might not ever see her again and…I don't know…it just…cracked. I thought everyone in Rakgar's lair heard it. That's why I ran out."

"Wow!" Anna whispered. She peered around Hiro to ogle Tog's heart in his claw. "Where did you get it?"

He yanked it sharply from view again. "None of your business, human!" he snapped at her.

"Go, Tog," Hiro said to him. "She's a worthy dame." Tog momentarily forgot the obnoxious human. "Go," Hiro repeated. "Give it to her before we leave."

With half a grin and a nod, Tog rushed out of the cave entrance, not stopping to look back.

"What was that nonsense about?" Anna asked when he'd left.

"Tog has chosen a mate," Hiro told her. "He goes to offer her his heart."

"His heart?" Anna's shoulders wilted. Hiro almost laughed at the confused look on her face. "Do you mean figuratively or literally?"

"Both." He returned to his sleeping spot.

After a moment's thought, Anna followed him. "You mean that gem he was holding?" She pointed her little finger after Tog. "That was his heart?"

Hiro nodded. Before the woman sat down he huddled her with his claw to situate her between himself and the wall, blocking her from view of the entrance to his cave. "A dan's heart can break only once."

"A dan?" she asked, seating herself.

"A male dragon."

"Oh."

"A dan's heart is cordate."

She tilted her head. "It's what?"

"Cordate." He dragged a claw across the ground to draw a picture. "Heart-shaped. When it breaks," he drew a line down the middle of the heart on the ground, "half of it is disgorged in the shape of a teardrop, like you saw."

"Will she give him her heart, too?" the woman asked with a wondering gaze.

Hiro shook his head. "Only a dan's heart breaks for his mate. A dame is free to fall in and out of love, just like a faerie."

"So she'll only accept it if she's also in love with him?"

Another nod. "Exactly. Now you see why he's so nervous about it."

Anna shrugged. "Does he have to give it to her?"

Hiro shook his head. "No, but he'll always be drawn to her, wishing for her to reciprocate his affections. Besides, if he doesn't, they can't turn it into an egg."

Her eyes widened. "Will they do that today?"

Hiro frowned at her. "That's a very intimate question. I know Tog very well and I don't think even I would be so bold as to ask him."

"I'm sorry." She studied the ground. "I don't know the culture of dragons." She shrugged her shoulders. "No human does."

"I thought humans took it upon themselves to beat answers out of anything they didn't understand," he said.

She gave him a disapproving grimace. "Apparently neither of us knows very much about the other. But at least I'm willing to learn."

5

NAYSAYERS

Philip focused on the sword swinging toward him, concentrating past the clamorous ringing through the arena while he practiced with Torgon. Tommak, the general who commanded the captains within Kingstor, sat on a stone bench nearby. Ten generals commanded the ten provinces of the Noble Kingdom. The population of Kingstor was such that it required its own general while the king and his castle always retained its own Royal General and guards.

Each general, including Torgon, took charge of ten captains. Each captain commanded ten lieutenants, but each lieutenant could command up to one hundred guards. They rarely needed so many, but in times of war they tried to recruit as many as they could, or so Philip had been trained. However, with the Treaty of the Swords, Avonoa had not seen human war in several centuries.

Promotions were also rare. Not only did a man have to pass a test of swordsmanship and a test of strategy, but he also had to pay a tribute to the testers. Therefore usually only the wealthy men could gain much rank.

For this session, a few generals from areas not too far away came to practice alongside and with the king. Their idea of practice, however, was to stand around critiquing the younger men on moves they themselves could no longer execute. Riddig was one of these generals.

Riddig came from his province, bringing Murzod as ordered. Torgon had warned Philip that Murzod would be present today, so they both made a point to completely ignore him. Months ago Murzod had made the mistake of attempting to manipulate a bad situation into a promotion to Royal General for himself by mistreating Torgon, who was only a lieutenant at the time. Not only had Torgon's exceptional behavior won him his current promotion, but Murzod's crude demeanor lost him two full ranks. Now the lieutenant created more trouble than he ever did as general, so Philip began to question the necessity for that demotion in the first place. Torgon asked one of his captains to assign Murzod some menial task such as gate duty or tower patrol to keep him out of trouble. But today was his rotation for sword practice.

While Philip and Torgon were sparring, Philip felt the sting of Bragon's absence. Bragon had always thrown out tips and comments as Philip sparred, but today the generals said nothing of his performance or Torgon's. Eventually, after Torgon unarmed him for what felt like the millionth time, Philip called for a rest. Torgon resumed his attack with the next man in line.

The sharp clang of swords echoed through the arena. Being a spacious area under the castle overlooking part of the city, part of the forest and the royal stables between the two, the arena could accommodate hundreds of practicing guards. Because of the rain in fall, the king and his guards rarely had more onlookers than just the stable boys. With thousands of tons of brick and stone overhead and only a smattering of rough columns supporting the area, Philip had often wondered when he was a boy what would happen should some of those columns crack. Eventually, he assumed it had been built with majik.

Seating himself next to Tommak, Philip shook a weary arm at Torgon, "What do you think of my Royal General, Tommak?"

Philip had always liked Tommak. He was a tall, broad man with a flat nose and shiny, bald head. He had been bald for as long as Philip could remember, but never seemed a day older. Philip remembered when he was a child how Tommak, then a captain, often slipped him candy behind Bragon's and his father's backs. Philip never knew if the man did it simply to be in his good graces, but the kindness always felt genuine.

"He's a good choice," Tommak answered, handing Philip a cloth. "I think our new king is wise beyond his years."

"You aren't bitter you didn't get the appointment yourself, then?" Philip asked with caution while wiping his brow.

"Let's be honest," Tommak grinned and looked at Philip with sly eyes. "I didn't want the responsibility."

Philip grinned back. "Besides," Tommak raised his voice to a more conversational level, "it's important to have the best swordsman of the kingdom defending the king. Bragon always told me that's why he kept Torgon stationed at the castle."

"Are you sure it wasn't simply because he wanted to keep an eye on him?" Philip questioned, although he doubted it.

"It's actually rather rare for a father to command his own son," Tommak said. "Some guards might cry favoritism while the son might cry foul. But Bragon and Torgon never fell victim to either."

Philip took a flagon of cold water offered him by a servant and said, "I believe that. Bragon was always a logical man and Torgon is very much like his father. But do you think I should've chosen someone who had at least passed the General Trials?"

Tommak narrowed his eyes at Philip turning slightly to face him. "But," Tommak hesitated, "Torgon *has* passed the trials. Surely you know—"

Philip narrowed his eyes. "Know what?"

Tommak shifted on the bench they occupied, allowing his eyes to drift to Riddig and Xiddick who sat a few hand lengths behind Philip. He sat up straighter. "Torgon passed the General Swordsmanship and Strategy Trials not six months ago. He has won every tournament he's ever entered." Philip turned back to see his Royal General unarm another man with a grin before returning his weapon to him.

"Then why wasn't he already a captain?" Philip asked.

Tommak's eyes drifted again to Riddig and Xiddick. "There were some who thought the promotion … er …premature," he said carefully.

Philip angled his head in time to see Riddig shift away in his peripheral vision. Philip stared into Tommak's face then threw his eyes over his shoulder to indicate the two generals. Tommak took a deep breath and dipped his head ever so slightly as he sighed.

Just as he had begun to cool down, heat washed over Philip that had nothing to do with his exertions. Philip had felt a natural suspicion of people since birth. When he was young he thought the servants whispered behind their hands about him. He constantly fought a war within himself in order to trust anyone around him. It was something he worked on with Murthur for many years, not only learning to trust the people around him, but also learning to tell the difference between his own suspicions and real threats.

Now Philip put his lessons learned into practice. He felt the suspicions growing stronger, but tried to look at the situation logically. Would Riddig and Xiddick stand to gain anything from keeping Torgon at a low station? Possibly their own appointments and promotions for their friends. More tribute from trials repeated? Could there be an explanation for their actions? Did they simply believe him too young? Did they not trust him? None of those seemed likely, but there might be another explanation.

Bragon had warned him that some of the generals would side with the nobles should they decide to usurp the throne before Philip could gain it. He knew Riddig would be one of them. The man was power hungry. He hadn't retired his commission even though he was well on in years. Could Tommak possibly be lying about the facts? Could he have it wrong? Neither of those seemed likely, either. He would have to discuss it further with Torgon and possibly Tommak, too.

"Well," Philip finally forced himself to smile. "It seems all the more important to keep him by my side in these dangerous times." He stood. "Torgon," he called to his friend, wanting to change the subject, "I think we'll discuss this now."

Torgon nodded his head and allowed a captain to take over for him. Philip called the generals over. In all, only Torgon, Tommak, Riddig, Xiddick and a general from the coastline named Iddialo were present. "I have an important mission to assign to one of our number," he said to them. "Important, but extremely dangerous." As he spoke he could see some of the captains and lieutenants slow their swords to listen. "I need to send a captain, ten lieutenants and fifty staff guards to the Great Northern Mountain with the faeries. Conditions will be brutal and they'll be under the command of the faeries. I need recommendations for captains who—"

"I'll do it!" Philip heard a yell from behind a few captains. He couldn't tell who said it until the man came forward. Then he recognized him. "Please, Sire." Gravel crunched when Murzod fell to his knees in front of Philip, who gave Torgon a withering look. Philip well remembered Murzod's beady eyes and pointed nose, but the man had allowed a scruffy beard to cover his chin while the black and white speckled hair on top of his head thinned. "Please, I know I've disappointed you before, Your Majesty. Allow me to redeem myself in your service."

"I need a captain, Lieutenant." Philip answered, but Riddig stepped forward.

"I would certainly support a field promotion for this circumstance, Sire." He gestured toward the penitent Murzod. "I probably would've recommended Lieutenant Murzod be included in the party as it was."

Philip's suspicions lifted the hair on his neck, but he did his best to ignore it. "I'll take it under consideration. The rest of you will please submit names for recommendation by the end of the day."

The generals nodded and turned back to their "practice." Philip faced Torgon, who turned his back to Murzod. Murzod stood and slowly returned to his own sparring.

Torgon removed his gloves and slapped them into his hand. "I don't like it," he said before Philip could ask. "He's too eager to please."

"Is that a bad thing?" Philip asked.

"You've heard the complaints from the villagers who've dealt with him," he said. "I've heard that and worse about him from those too afraid to complain."

"Recently?"

Torgon reluctantly shook his head. "Before my most recent appointment."

Philip examined the men. He watched Murzod, but looked away before his gaze was returned. "To be truthful," he said, "If a vengeance-crazed dragon is on its way to Kingstor to rip out my throat, I'd prefer to have those I trust most surrounding me." Torgon grinned at this, but had the modesty to look away. "Let's allow him the opportunity to 'redeem' himself as he asks, and keep our best men from having to do the dangerous work. Besides, if anyone can manage him, it would be the faeries."

6

OUT OF THE CLOUDS

For once, Hiro loathed the darkness. He grimaced as he stared out his cave entrance. Only a few other dragons flew through the pouring fall rains; most seemed to avoid the weather. He knew The Watch would be hidden among the rocky crags under the floating mountains. The rain fell at a steady patter, but not nearly as torrential as it had been before nightfall. All the same, the cloud cover made the darkness absolute.

"You'll have to curl up in my claw," he whispered.

"I'll be fine," Anna grumbled.

"It won't feel like a feather bed," Tog told her. He had returned a short time ago after giving his heart to Surneen. She accepted it without a blink of the eye. Hiro was happy for his friend. To find a mate was a necessary step in life, but Hiro hoped to put it off as long as possible.

"I haven't slept in feather beds all my life," she snapped back. "I'm more hardened than either of you might expect."

"Oh, indeed," Tog said. "You're brave enough to trick a dragon into doing what you want. I'll tell you this," he stepped closer to her. "If it had been any other dragon, you'd be dead. You're lucky it was me that found you."

She opened her mouth to retort, but Hiro quieted them by snarling, "It's time to leave."

Hiro scooped Anna into his claw. At first she sat cradled in his fist, but then she pulled her hair under her chin and tucked her many folds of skirt around her knees. Though she was normally tall for a human, though slender, Hiro marveled how small she could be when she trussed herself together.

He tucked her further under his front leg joint where it met his body. "Hopefully anyone who sees us will think I'm just bringing along extra food for the journey."

"It's better than the branches Tog bundled me in to bring me here," the woman said before folding herself up entirely.

"That was to keep you controlled. I had no idea what you might do," Tog said, crawling up next to them. Then he added to Hiro, "I hope she doesn't get us killed."

"If we're caught with her," Hiro said, "we'll just eat her."

A muffled "Ha ha ha" came from the bundle under his front leg.

Launching themselves into the black sky, they sheered under the Rock Clouds. Hiro twisted his neck around to gaze upon his floating cave before it rose out of sight. His heart clenched in his chest. He'd hoped never to leave his home again. Now he abandoned it with a human curled beneath him.

They decided to drop straight down to get under The Watch as quickly as possible, but as they skimmed the Inner Mountain gliding under the floating mountains, they heard a call behind them. "Good luck, Hiro!" Prak's voice echoed behind them.

"Stupid hatchling," Hiro muttered. And they flew on.

When they had flown a few wingfalls, Hiro snaked his neck around to look behind them. With a brief glance at Tog, who just rolled his eye, Hiro loosened Anna from under his leg joint. "Ugh," she groaned as she uncurled, "dragon armpit."

She sat in his claw, clinging to his wrist with her arms, as he hung it in a curve. He mostly protected her from the rain with his body, but she still got sprayed with water as they flew. "How far is it to the faerie shaman?" she asked, squinting toward the horizon.

"I would guess three days," Hiro said.

"Guess?" She sat up straighter. "Guess? You don't know?"

"Well, I've never been there before," he said. Out of the corner of his eye he saw Tog watching him. Turning to his friend, Tog shook his head wide-eyed.

"But you know how to get there?" the woman persisted.

"Of course I do," Hiro said. Tog continued to shake his head.

"I don't understand," she said. "Did someone tell you how to get there, but not how far it was?"

"Rakgar showed me the way." As soon as Hiro said it, Tog dropped his head with a sigh. He was surprised Tog didn't groan.

"Showed you?" Anna said, wiping water from her face. "How can he show you the way? Have you been there or not?"

Hiro beat his wings and shifted his limbs. He didn't know if he should tell her this or not. Of course, he should never have admitted to being able to speak in the first place. This was all new sky.

"Well?" she asked again, a little sharper.

"Don't," Tog said at his side.

"Don't what?" Anna said through a clenched jaw. "What are you talking about?"

Hiro sighed, throwing more rain over Anna. "There are a great many things we'll have to explain to her, Tog."

The woman looked between the two dragons, but waited. Hiro thought it a wise decision on her part.

Tog hissed at her then beat his wings to push himself ahead of them. Or to throw more rain over the pair, Hiro couldn't decide which.

Hiro twisted his head to look down on Anna. "There are many things you don't understand about dragons."

"Then tell me," she said. "There's no better way to forge a friendship than to attempt to understand someone."

"Even if that someone might eat you?" Hiro returned at her. He heard Tog snort from in front of them.

Anna put one fist on her hip, but used the other arm to keep her grasp on his leg. "You're not as ruthless as you'd like to be and I know it." Hiro grinned, but when he didn't respond, she coaxed further. "So how do you know where we're going? *If* you know."

He sighed again and rolled his shoulder. "Dragons can pass memories to each other in our breath. Rakgar passed me a memory of how to get to the faerie shaman and what the creature looks like."

"Incredible," Anna whispered.

"This rain is miserable," Tog moaned, clearly anxious to change the topic. He dropped back to Hiro's side. "Are we far enough away?"

"Let's try it!" Hiro pounded the rain back with his wings and Tog followed.

"Try what?" Anna asked, but cut off when Hiro angled upward and she was forced to fling both arms around his leg to keep from falling.

"Trust me," he answered. The black and gray dragons pulsed their wings as they rose into the torrent. Harder and harder they pressed. Anna clung tighter as they lifted into the clouds. She made a noise that sounded like a snort of indignation, but Hiro kept his eyes ahead to avoid flashes of lightning.

They continued on their northwest course but angled upward. It would take effort to get above the clouds but it would shorten their flight time to avoid currents and storms. Flying above the clouds was always easier, it just took some time to get there. A human wouldn't know anything about it.

Hiro felt the clouds around him. The blackness roiled with shimmers of lightning. Inside a rain cloud could be a dangerous place. The pair pressed harder. Finally Hiro felt the tops of the clouds ahead. Anna made a strange noise into the scales against his leg, but before he could ask what she wanted he was distracted when they broke through the clouds.

Anna's grip on Hiro's leg vanished entirely when they peeked through the clouds to see the three moons of Avonoa hanging over them, surrounded by millions of the centaurs' precious stars. Some stars clustered in groups like blinking jewelry, others stretched across the night sky in scattered layers, but all dazzled the tops of the storm clouds below. Hiro stared around them in wonder at the sight.

"Didn't I tell you to trust me?" he whispered into the vast beauty before them. "Flying will be much easier up here." When the human didn't respond, he curved his neck and jerked his head to peer closer at her.

She slumped in his claw, eyes closed and mouth hanging open. "Anna?" He twitched his claw to shake her, but without her own firm grasp around his leg, she slipped. "Anna!" he yelled. The little princess slid further to dangle by her skirt from just two of his talons. He grabbed for her with the other claw, but missed. The frail human fell and disappeared into the storm clouds below.

7

TALENTS

With a roar and no backward glance at Tog, Hiro plunged after her. Diving through the clouds, he saw Anna below him, contorting falling feet over head. His tail strained against the storm to keep him on course. Thunder shook the cloud around them, but the lightning kept her in Hiro's view. Tucking his wings, he plummeted toward her. Suddenly, with her skirt around her head he saw her legs kick. Her arms shoved the clothing down to emit a scream. She continued to keel until Hiro tucked her into all four claws. Spreading his wings again, he caught an upward draft to slow their descent, but trembled with the violence of the storm.

"What happened?" she yelled with accusation over the drumming thunder.

"How should I know, you're the one who fell asleep!"

"Fell asleep?" She squirmed as he passed her back into his claw. "All I remember is you flying up into the clouds like a mad dragon and I couldn't breathe and then…then falling!"

"She falls forward," Tog's voice came from overhead. "I'll give her that."

"I couldn't breathe!" she yelled. "I couldn't even tell you I couldn't breathe!"

Hiro twisted to look at Tog. "I don't think we'll be flying above the storms on this journey."

"It will take at least half a day longer to go through them," Tog grumbled.

Hiro rolled his shoulder. "It seems humans can't breathe above the clouds."

"Interesting to know," Tog growled again, "but this human is slowing us down."

"I'm sorry," thunder punctuated Anna's voice, "there's no way I could've known."

"There's no way any of us could've known," Hiro echoed, "but it will be a long, wet journey from here."

They flew in silence awhile longer. Occasionally Tog would cast a measured glance up into the rain, glare at Hiro, then push ahead of them again.

Anna shivered in his claw. Wrapping one arm around her legs and keeping an extra tight grip with the other arm on Hiro's leg, eventually she muttered, "Any majikal means of keeping a freezing human warm?"

"Other than fire?"

She actually harrumphed at him.

But Hiro noticed how she shivered in his claw. "My body temperature doesn't keep you warm?" he asked.

"Yes and no," she said as her jaw rattled. "The p-part of me against you is warm, but the rest of me is exposed and soaked to the skin. S-sort of like sitting beside a fire; one side is warm, but the other side is c-cold. And the side next to you doesn't dry."

"We'll be flying through rain for three days," he said. "What would you suggest to keep yourself alive?"

"Flying in the d-day, for one," she stuttered.

"Not always possible, if we want to hurry."

"Possibly an animal s-skin, for another," she forced through chattering teeth.

"We won't carry along provisions for you. We're not pack animals," Tog said from ahead of them, then he dropped back on a current of air to fly beside Hiro again. "And we need to keep the talking to a minimum. We're flying just above the forest; we don't want any *more* humans to hear us speak."

"I can understand the need for silence, but cold can k-kill humans faster than dragons." Her eyes drifted up to Hiro again. "And humans need to eat more often."

Tog rolled his eyes and groaned. Pressing against the current again, he flew ahead. For good measure he shook the rain off, sending it splashing onto Hiro. Hiro just sighed. "How often do humans need to eat?"

"Normally," the woman answered as she wiped water from her face with the bottom of her dress, "humans eat three times a day—"

"Three times!" Tog interrupted. "We'll never get there!"

"—but," she shouted louder, "I can suffice with o-one."

"We'll dry some meat for you to carry with us," Hiro said. "That way we won't have to stop. And we can salvage the hide to cover you."

Anna curled tighter into a ball. "H-how soon can we do this?"

Hiro lifted his head. The temperature dropped steadily and he knew it would continue to drop for at least the next two days. He sighed again, rolling his shoulder. Tog wouldn't be happy. "We'll keep an eye out for prey."

As they flew through the inky night, Hiro noticed Anna shivering more and more violently in his claw. She tried to roll from side to side. She tried to curl into a ball, but for some reason she couldn't stay in one place. Hiro tried to pull her closer to his side to keep her warm, but she couldn't get comfortable. Finally, Hiro called to Tog.

"We need to find some kind of animal hide for her," he told his friend.

"We're not even halfway through the night," Tog called back. "How is she going to survive the entire flight?"

"I'm sure the hide will help," Hiro answered, although he wasn't completely sure himself.

Tog rolled his eyes, knowing Hiro couldn't see much of anything in the dark, but the two dragons found an open space to land in the forest beneath. Once their feet were on the ground, they both stopped. Not an eyelid flickered or a single scale slithered. Only the drip of the constant flow of rain on bare branches could be heard.

"What's the matter?" Anna whispered. She made an attempt to move from Hiro's claw, but he held her fast.

After a moment, Hiro looked at Tog and nodded. Then he allowed the human to slide to the ground. "We were just checking for danger," he told her.

"Oh." She peered into the dark trees around them. "And?"

"I don't hear or smell anything nearby," he whispered.

Anna nodded. "Now what?"

"You'll stay here with Tog—"

"But—" Tog started.

"Don't argue," Hiro snapped. "I'm the better hunter and you know it."

Tog snorted and flopped to the ground. "Don't expect me to cuddle you, human," he huffed. "I don't care if you freeze to death."

Anna curled onto the ground, shivering as she sat, so Hiro broke a branch from a tree, poured flame over it and tossed it in front of her. Every time a raindrop fell into the flames, a spark shot out. "Won't the rain put it out?" she asked.

"Eventually," he said, "but dragon fire is more resistant than any other. You should be fine until I return."

"And what will you hunt?" she asked. "You said nothing is nearby?"

"My sense of smell will guide me," he told her. "I'll try to find a lydik if I can. The hairy hide would be more than enough to keep you warm."

"And lydik meat is delicious," Tog mumbled.

"And the stomach of a lydik is an excellent water bag," Anna added.

Even Tog turned his long neck to look at her. "How on this green world could you know that?" he asked.

Anna put her nose in the air. "There are a great many things you don't know about me, either."

"Then," said Hiro, "I'll bring the whole animal back and you can tell us more."

With that, he left the two brooding creatures behind him as he lumbered into the woods. He hoped the human would still be alive when he returned.

Hiro sniffed the sodden ground. Rain always seemed to wash away scents, but after smelling a few arcs across the forest floor, he found a meager scent of dirt, grass and rotten berries—the unmistakable scent of lydik. Very faint, but present nonetheless. Following it dozens of dragon lengths away, he found a few of the wandering beasts. The best huntress wouldn't have found such a trail. He jumped out and severed the throat of one with his saber-sharp talons. Careful not to put any holes in the hide, he carried it back to the others.

"It must be one of the first few wandering in this area for the season," he said, returning to his companions.

"That's not likely," Anna said, looking the creature over. "Their coarse fur allows them to wander year round. Cut it apart along here, if you please." She indicated where Hiro should slice with his talons.

After he had done so, Anna picked up a sharp-edged rock and began digging at the edges of the hide, efficiently peeling it away from the muscle beneath. As she worked, Tog wandered over to watch.

"You could challenge Priya with your talent at peeling an animal," he muttered. The woman fumbled and dropped the rock, but picked it back up and narrowed her eyes at Tog.

When Tog ignored her curious look, Anna directed it to Hiro. "Who is this Priya, anyway? Is she your mate, Hiro?"

"It's only a matter of time," Tog mumbled. Noticing Hiro's pursed lips, Tog changed the subject. "How do you know how to do this?" he asked, indicating the dead animal again, as blood soaked her sleeves. "I thought human princesses never got their hands dirty in your world."

"Ordinarily, we don't," she said, shaking pieces from her fingers. "But I wasn't raised as a princess. I was brought up in the mountains by an old woman named Sar. She taught me how to hunt, cook, clean, plant, ride a horse, even wield a sword—along with teaching me how to be a noblewoman." She easily pulled the hide from the animal and held it up to Hiro. "You don't, by chance, know how to tan, do you?" she asked.

"Tan?"

"I thought not." She pointed to the fleshy inside of the skin. "Just dry it the way you would the meat."

Hiro laid it across his claws with the fur side down. He breathed out hot air, much the way he might send a memory, but with a lick of flame inside his nostrils much too hot for a memory. When he had covered it, he stopped and handed it back to her.

She wrapped it around her shoulders and sighed. "That will do wonders." She pulled the hide from the head of the lydik over her own head and tied the two front legs together in front of her to keep it on. Then she set to work on the meat with the rock.

"I'll do that part," Hiro said. "Just get the stomach and anything else you don't want burned."

She pulled the stomach away, cutting off the top and bottom tubes with the rock. She deftly turned the stomach inside out and wiped off the contents with the help of the sprinkle of rain falling. She turned it back around and cauterized the bottom tube with the flame clinging stubbornly to the branch Hiro had provided her.

"If there was a water source nearby you could fill it," Hiro said, inspecting her work.

Anna glanced around them then answered, "No need." She stepped between two large trees and tore a chunk of moss from the ground. "Hytocomp," she said as she squeezed the moss over the opening. A surprising amount of water rushed from the plant into the bag. "It soaks up the rain in fall and disperses it throughout the year to the surrounding plants. Farmers use it to keep their fields from flooding and it grows common enough everywhere." As she said the last, she moved to another clump of moss and began pulling it up.

Anna went about her work and Hiro turned back to the carcass. He breathed hot air on it, the same way he had on the skin, with only a small flame within his nostrils. The muscle of the pig-like animal sizzled and steamed. As it cooked, the meat pulled away from the bone of its own accord. He rolled it over to get both sides. After just a few minutes all that remained was a pile of bones with clumps of dried meat on top and wedged between.

Tog paced a large circle around them as Anna gathered the meat. Again she surprised the dragons by taking up a large portion of it, but also including the innards. She used the dried intestines to bundle together the heart, all three livers and even the triple-chambered lungs. "I thought humans didn't eat the wealth," Hiro said, referring to the dragons' name for an animal's organs.

"They're not preferred," Anna said, "but I'm perfectly aware of the nutrition. And I've heard that the Sing Bladder is a delicacy among certain tribes in the Just Kingdom." Hiro shook his head and inspected the wet sky.

"Should we just stay here for the night?" Tog asked. "We've wasted a good piece of it anyway."

"Perhaps it would be best," Hiro answered. He could feel the clouds thickening overhead. The air raised his scales as he knew it would for Tog. "We'll have to sleep under the trees. A storm is coming."

8

COURAGE OF MEN

The messenger laid another report on the war table and saluted, then exited the room. Philip and Torgon hovered over the large table in the council chamber where they had previously met Qialla for the first time. Philip had specifically requested a smaller fire in the grate because there were no windows to open for ventilation, but the stifling heat seemed to come from the opposite side of the room where the faeries stood, watching from the corner. Philip had called the faeries in to consult with them on the reports Torgon had gathered, but they stayed silent and watched.

The table was no longer empty, as when they first greeted the faeries. Now it was strewn with papers of reports of a black creature attacking villages and the numbers of people and animals killed. It also held three different maps, all at the same orientation—one that included all of Avonoa, one of the Courageous Kingdom and one of the Noble Kingdom. Golden disc weights held down the curled edges except on the northwestern-most edge of the Noble Kingdom map and the southeastern edge of the Courageous Kingdom map.

Philip made no move as Torgon picked up the latest report and consulted the map. He rolled down the edge of the Courageous Kingdom map and pointed at it. "Dakben."

"How many?" Philip asked.

Torgon hesitated only a moment. "Twenty-two, not including livestock."

Philip shook his head at Torgon's finger placement. "Then it continues to move away from Kingstor Courageous," he said.

"So it would seem," Torgon answered.

"It appears to be moving toward Kingstor Noble."

Torgon slid his finger a little further southwest. "The mountains might change its course."

"A dragon's course doesn't change easily." Kradik's voice came from the corner. "Mountains won't delay its justice."

Torgon only spared the faerie a fleeting glance before switching to a second paper that had been delivered with the report. "King Torodov," he told Philip, "has ordered his people to evacuate its path up to the Torthoth Mountains at the edge of his kingdom. Obviously everyone won't leave. He says if his people decide to stay, they take their lives in their own hands, but he refuses to send men to our kingdom or try to stop the beast in any way."

"I thought the Courageous Kingdom was made of courageous men?" Philip said, still staring at the map.

"Torodov and his generals claim bravery has nothing to do with stupidity." Torgon crumpled the paper and threw it aside.

Philip nodded. "Make sure we have fresh sentries along the route to the Torthoth Mountains. I want to know as soon as this monster enters the Noble Kingdom."

"We'll need more men in the north."

"Gather five captains and their men from southern provinces," he said. "The people there shouldn't be in danger, so they'll support the northern captains." Philip took a deep breath then forced his eyes to the faeries. "Is there no way to surprise this beast, like the dragons before?"

"It would not have the same effect, I'm afraid," Kradik said.

"Besides," Qialla continued, "we can't do anything until we have the poison. I'm sure the King's Guard are strong enough to fight without our assistance for the time being."

Philip turned back to Torgon in time to see his jaw unclench. "Send as many men as you can from the south. Perhaps we can overwhelm it as soon as it crosses the mountains."

"Yes, Sire." Torgon saluted and left the room.

Philip straightened to face Kradik once the door closed behind his general. "The men and supplies for your expedition will be ready to leave soon," he told the faerie.

Kradik responded with a small bow and followed Torgon out of the chamber. After they left, Qialla stepped forward. "If you can hold off one dragon until we're more prepared, we'll rain destruction on all dragons in answer for every death of faerie or human."

Philip released his breath hoping it sounded like relief. Leaning his knuckles on the table, in his mind he grumbled, *that's what I'm afraid of.*

A GAME

"You'll fly in silence like this all day?" Anna finally spoke into the quiet falling rain.

Hiro glanced at Tog, who rolled his eye. "It is preferable to humans discovering our secret," Hiro rumbled into the misty sky. The storm had been severe during the night, but gave way to a foggy morning.

Anna gave an exaggerated sigh. "But it's boring for those of us traveling with you. All I have to do all day is wipe water from my face."

"At least you can eat," Hiro said.

"I know what we can do," Tog said suddenly. Even Anna jerked at the playful tone in his voice, so opposing to his recent demeanor.

With caution, Hiro asked, "What's that?"

"We could have a game of Catch It." Tog's smile betrayed him. "You made a wonderful catch last night. Now give me a turn."

"What's 'Catch It'?" Anna asked.

Tog grinned at her. "It's wonderful! We throw something from a great height and race to see who can catch it soonest. Hiro, you throw her and I'll see if I can catch her."

With Tog's eye on her, Anna thrust her arms around Hiro's leg clasping her hands around it. Hiro lifted her to his eye level. She squeaked when he gave her a little shake. "I don't think Anna's up for that game," Hiro said, then swung Anna back down below him.

Tog pushed ahead of them again, grumbling over his shoulder, "Then don't complain about being bored."

After flying in silence awhile, Hiro struck on an idea. "Riddles!" he said. Tog's head twitched to the side. He knew he could tempt Tog with riddles. "We could toss some riddles."

"'Toss riddles'?" Anna asked. "What does that mean?"

Tog circled around beside them again. "I don't think she's up for that game, either," he said. "She can't even figure out what it means to 'toss riddles.'"

Hiro shook his head, "It just means to guess riddles," he told her. "Like throwing them back and forth at each other. Except throwing these won't hurt anyone."

"I love riddles," she said. "I've just never heard it described that way before."

"Okay," Hiro said, "I'll go first."

"You forget yourself," Tog interrupted, "we should be silent."

Hiro waved off his friend. "No one on the ground will imagine they're hearing anything from the sky. They'll just think they heard someone passing by, playing a human riddle game." He stuck out his chin. "Do humans play riddle games?" he asked Anna.

"Of course," she smirked. "We just don't call it 'tossing riddles.'"

"Alright," Hiro nodded, "I'll start with an easy one for the human." He pursed his lips together to think. "What asks, but never answers?"

"Oh, no," Tog groaned. "We're not going to make it this easy, are we? It won't be any fun at all."

"An owl!" Anna squeaked. "Give me a harder one, then, Tog."

Tog thought for a moment and grinned. "Many have heard me, but nobody has seen me, and I will not speak back until spoken to."

"I thought you said you would give her a difficult one," Hiro muttered.

"An echo!" Anna said from beneath. "My turn." She thought for a moment, wiping rain from her face again. "When you need me, you throw me away. But when you're done with me, you bring me back."

The two dragons stared at each other. Then Tog glanced at Anna. Hiro's brow creased as he grimaced straight ahead.

"Well?" the woman asked. "Come on, this is an easy one."

Tog looked back to Hiro, then turned his focus ahead and glared into the rain. "She's better than I thought," he mumbled.

Hiro rolled his shoulder, realizing his friend would never concede. "Alright, I drop. What is it?"

"Drop?" Anna squirmed, throwing her arms around his leg again.

"Yes, drop," Hiro nodded. "We're tossing riddles and I dropped it. What is it?"

"Oh," she said, "it's an anchor."

The dragons eyed each other again. Tog nodded, "I should've known a human would cheat. What's an anchor?"

"What's an—? Are you playing another game with me?" She tilted her head toward Tog. "You don't know what—? Oh—no—I guess you wouldn't, would you? Alright," she wiped her face again, "let me try another one. How many—" she stopped. "No, you wouldn't know that one, either."

Anna fell into muttering to herself. The dragons rolled their eyes at each other. They often heard the words "too human" and "narrow-minded."

"Ah!" she finally yelled. "I've got one! What's the most common use for a lydik hide?"

"A blanket for a little princess," Tog grinned at her.

"That's the second most common," she grinned with sly eyes at him.

"Something else only humans would do?" Hiro asked with a smirk of his own.

"No," she shook her head and folded her arms.

"Food?" Hiro asked.

Anna shrugged, "For you, maybe."

"Alright," Tog answered after another moment. "I drop."

"To keep a lydik warm, of course."

Tog narrowed his eyes at Hiro. "Drop her."

Their game continued for some time. Anna discarded more riddles than she used, but took her turns in stride. After a while, Hiro noticed Anna's riddles coming slower and being easier. However, he hadn't noticed the darkening clouds. Suddenly lightning shook the world directly over their heads. Hiro's scales rose at the presence of a treacherous storm surrounding them.

"Follow me!" Tog yelled. Heavy drops slapped them as if diving into a waterfall. Boiling black clouds battered the creatures fighting their way through the violent sky. Hiro followed his friend, dipping into the trees beneath. Slipping through the branches, he pulled Anna close to his chest without thinking.

Once under the pines, the beating rain eased, but still poured. After checking for safety, Hiro looked down at the soggy human in his fist. She hunched under the hairy animal skin with her eyes half-closed. "Do you think you'll be able to sleep here?" Hiro asked Anna. He only partially cared. She had no other choice.

She lurched away and fell to the ground. "No feather bed necessary," she mumbled, pulling her lydik hide back over her head.

Tog and Hiro curled on the ground on either side of her. "I'm guessing the sun is well up," Tog told Hiro in a low voice. The storm clouds made everything so dark they could only guess. "Thank Kruh the storm will ease soon."

"Kruh?" Anna mumbled. "Why would you be thankful to the god of the clouds?" She used her right hand to swipe each shoulder, then squirmed further into her covering.

"As harsh as the storms of fall can be," Tog said, "you should be thankful to Kruh for having a respite."

After a moment of silence, Hiro couldn't help himself. "Anna," he whispered as low as the pattering rain would allow. Receiving a grunt of reply, he knew she was still awake. "Why do humans do that?" he asked. "Brushing off the shoulders, I mean. I saw some of the men doing it while I was captured, but I don't understand it."

"To keep evil from clinging to us," came the muffled response. She lifted the hide to peer out at him. "They probably saw a black dragon as an evil omen. Bad luck might follow." Replacing the hide, she said, "I can see why, now."

Tog growled, "If we are such evil omens perhaps we should leave you here."

"Or perhaps I should walk!" Her voice sounded almost like a dragon's. She threw the hide from over her head and perched on an elbow. "I can't get a moment's comfort on this cold ground!" She jerked her chin to Hiro, who flinched from the look in her eye. "Can I lie next to you?" She struggled to soften her tone. "I could use some extra warmth."

Hiro lifted an eyebrow to Tog, but his friend grimaced and turned away. Hiro rolled his shoulder before answering. "If you can stand the bad luck that might rub off on you."

—

The rain did ease later and the trio slept a few hours in relative peace. Lesser storms came, but Anna didn't complain. After a long while of listening to the rain drub his scales as if a circle of centaurs stood around him pounding drums, Hiro could take it no longer.

Lifting his head, he inspected the sky. It was as dark as it had been when they'd landed and the rain continued to pour. He had no way of knowing what time of day it was, but he didn't care. "Tog," he called, loud enough to rouse his two companions. When neither answered, he tried again. "Tog!" he practically yelled.

"I know," the gray lump next to him answered. Lifting his head, he blinked his protruding eyes awake. "Time to go." He motioned to the little human next to Hiro. "Can I wake her?"

"No," Anna said from under her blanket, but she didn't move.

When she didn't come out, Hiro replied, "Yes."

An evil grin spread across Tog's face as he lifted a claw toward her, but Anna threw back the hide. "I don't know which of you is worse." She pointed at Hiro, "The coward," then she turned her finger on Tog, "or the fiend."

Tog crooked a talon at her. "Ride with me today and you can find out."

"I may be human, but I'm not stupid," she shook her head.

"That remains to be seen," Tog said as Hiro opened his claw for Anna.

She stalled. "Actually, I'll need a moment before we can leave." Without another word, the woman ran into the forest and disappeared behind some trees.

"Now what?" Tog said falling back to the ground. "That woman is insufferable."

"You're just upset that you were outsmarted by a human," Hiro said, coiling his tail around himself.

"It's absolutely humiliating," Tog grumbled. "If anyone should ever find out…" He couldn't even finish the statement. He just growled and shook his head.

"You know I would never tell a soul," Hiro said.

"I know, but I don't like having her around." Tog tossed a withering look in the woman's direction. "She talks of bad luck and evil, with which I'm sure she's very friendly."

Hiro didn't know what to say. The human woman's presence didn't bother him. Dragons could usually sense danger, but Hiro felt none around her. In fact, he didn't mind having her around at all. Thinking about it, he felt a twinge of anger at himself.

Anna chose that moment to materialize from the trees, wrapping the animal hide around her shoulders.

"And what was that about?" Tog barked.

"Nothing," she said.

"Are we going to be stopping for 'nothing' often?" Tog retorted.

"No," she snapped. "Is it so horrible for me to have a few minutes to myself once a day?"

"I don't know," Tog scrooped, "I thought we were in a hurry to help the little princess."

Before stepping onto Hiro's claw, Anna spun to face Tog. "Hurry? I wouldn't know it from the way you old grandfathers fly."

Tog bared his fangs. "My name means 'fast'; you're the one holding us back."

"Tog—" Hiro tried to interrupt.

"Your name is supposed to mean 'fast'?" Anna hissed. "Did you name yourself?"

Tog twisted his neck away from her. "I don't have to listen to this."

Anna firmly put one fist on a hip. "Would you like to hear what I think your name should be?"

"Anna!" Hiro chided louder.

Tog snaked around to face her again, but Anna stood her ground. "I'd like to hear the sound of your bones crunching under my claw!"

"Why don't you just tuck your tail between your legs and run home, you coward?" she yelled up at him.

"It's physically impossible for a dragon to put its tail between its legs because dragons don't fear anything!"

He reached for her, but Hiro grabbed her around the waist and yanked her away. "We're wasting time!" Hiro bellowed.

Tog roared and leapt into the sky over Hiro's head. While she situated herself in his claw, Hiro shook his head. "I thought you were clever, but you must have completely lost your mind to get under the scales of a dragon."

———

After following Tog's tail in the air awhile, Anna shifted in Hiro's claw. "I suppose I should apologize," she tried to whisper.

Hiro shrugged, "It might make the journey a little easier."

"Doesn't he realize I'm making concessions, too?" Anna asked with uncertainty.

"Maybe," Hiro nodded, "but he'll never admit it."

"I guess I'll be the better…well…creature, then," she said. Hiro didn't respond. Finally, she called out. "Tog!" she yelled into the patter of rain on the gray dragon's back. "I'm sorry. I was being impatient and I apologize. I'm anxious for us to succeed and I know you are, too."

A moment later, Hiro gripped Anna and tilted his left wing up. Tog dropped back suddenly, but he didn't come level with Hiro. Instead, he leveled at Anna and swung his head within inches of hers. "Don't ever expect us to be friends, human. I should never have agreed to this." As quickly as he had dropped back, he pressed ahead again. Tog didn't speak the rest of the day.

10

SHA OGALALA KARPOO SHAMPEDER

"Praise Shurka! There it is!" Tog yelled over the pounding rain. Hiro squinted against the dark. They had been flying for three days with only occasional stops to sleep. The dark shroud of clouds persisted day and night.

Hiro had realized the night before the necessity of passing the directions to Tog. He told Anna it would be the prudent thing to do should something happen to him, but the real reason was that Hiro doubted his ability to see their nighttime course at all. Most dragons assumed because of his black scales Hiro had the most superior night vision of them all. That was the commonly held belief about black dragons, but in his case the opposite was true. Tog had far better eyesight in the dark than Hiro, but Tog was the only other being who knew that. Neither dragon would ever admit this to Anna. Hiro long ago insisted on Tog giving his wyrd never to reveal this secret to another soul.

Anna uncurled from her balled-up position in Hiro's claw. She pushed the hide away to peer through the darkness. "I don't see anything."

Hiro looked at Tog from the corner of his eye. When Tog nodded, Hiro played along. "Don't worry, we can see the faerie forest," Hiro told her.

Anna shrugged and again threw the hide over her head. She had eaten a good portion of the meat they'd acquired the first night of their trip, but plenty still remained. Hiro was surprised to see how much of it disappeared every day.

"How soon will we be there?" Anna's muffled voice asked.

She directed the question at Hiro, but Tog, with better night vision, was forced to answer first. "Only a few more hours, if I must guess. Hiro," Tog pointed his snout at Anna, "how will we explain that thing to the faerie?"

"We'll only tell her what she needs to know and make her give an oath first," Hiro said.

Anna sat up straight in Hiro's claw. "An oath? Will that stop her from telling anyone?"

Hiro nodded. "A faerie's oath is as serious as the wyrd of a dragon. We'll make her swear not to tell before she sees you, then she can't back out."

"The word of a dragon?" Anna snorted. "If a human gives his word it depends on the person whether or not they'll keep it."

"Yes, I've heard that the word of a human is as unbreakable as a dry twig," Tog mumbled.

Anna narrowed her eyes at him. "I said it depends on the person. I, for one, would never break my word. But there are, of course, untrustworthy humans. And faeries." The last remark she directed at Hiro.

"Tog knows how I feel about faeries," he told her. "He knows everything that happened to me. Now we need to keep quiet; we're entering faerie and human lands."

The trees here were not as tall as the Black Forest or those closer to the Rock Clouds, so the two dragons flew lower than normal. Hiro thought it prudent to keep the sound of their voices to a minimum. He didn't want to risk any other human wondering about them. Anna curled back into her ball.

The sky lightened with a thinning of the clouds as the two dragons began to drift in slow circles from the sky to the outer borders of the faerie forest of Shenharah. "Tog," Hiro kept his voice low. Both dragons knew from Rakgar's memory that no faeries but the shaman would be nearby. "Land in front of me. Keep her hidden."

Tog jerked his head. Hiro knew that, despite his misgivings, Tog would remain true. "Anna," he whispered to her as they grew closer to the ground, "stay behind Tog until the faerie takes the oath."

She bobbed her head, but whispered back, "She won't hurt me, will she?"

Hiro blinked at the fear in her voice. "Not while you're with us."

"Besides," Tog said, "if the faerie won't swear, I have another plan."

Hiro tilted his head toward Tog, "Oh?" he asked. "What's that?"

Tog swung his head to indicate Anna. "I'll eat her."

Moments later both dragons' feet touched the ground. They stood rock-still, peering into the darkness. Hiro closed his eyes, listening even closer. He mostly heard rain pattering among the trees, but he caught sounds of movement within a small hut only a few dragon lengths in front of them.

"She's inside," he whispered to Tog while laying Anna on the ground behind his gray friend. Anna stayed under the cover of the hide.

The faeries of Avonoa preferred to live in the trees among plants and animals; unlike the centaurs, who lived in the open fields and grasslands. Faerie shaman and lesser majishuns chose to live apart from others in order to practice their majik in relative quiet. The other faeries thought this wise because the experiments of majishuns could be fatal to anyone around them.

This shaman lived quite alone. Her home consisted of two small shelters built so close together that they leaned against each other. A thick thatch mixed with reddish mud topped the walls made of stacked stones. When dried with majikal means, the reddish mortar hardened to a nearly unbreakable substance.

But the hut wasn't the strangest sight to meet the travelers. Hanging among the trees were numerous totems and flags. Rough twigs, twisted and tied, hung from branches. Several indiscernible shapes and symbols were carved into tree trunks with colorful spikes surrounding them. Little upside-down pyramids of stone scattered around the clearing. Scraps of cloth had been tied to every single branch of three different trees. On only one of these trees, the flags fluttered as if in a wind but without a drop of rain on them. Fire smoke wafted through the trees, carrying with it the sour odor of a strange citrus. It must have been very strong indeed to manifest through the rain-saturated earth. The first snorks of fall left luminescent trails on a few of the tree trunks, but none of the trails ventured all the way up the trees as they normally would on other trees.

"Hello!" Hiro called. He paced out from behind Tog. The movements ceased within the little home. "Hiro Tekla Ido Tusten seeks a faerie shaman," he said over the noise of the rain.

The little wooden door at the front of the house creaked open. With the light of a fire burning behind her, Hiro could only see a faerie stooped with age. "Hiro Tekla," a gravelly voice answered. She sounded very similar to Visi. Did witches of every species have such voices? "I know no such person."

"I am no person." Hiro stepped closer to the faerie. Now he could see that this was the faerie shaman Rakgar had sent him to find. Long, white hair hung from the left side of her head while on the right side a tattoo of a snake wrapped its tail around her ear. The entire tattoo glowed in blues and greens like the snorks' trails. Three hairs as long as her arm jutted from her chin. In her own home, the faerie didn't wear the traditional cloaks and gloves they typically donned in front of humans. She wore nothing but a dirty blue cloth wrapped around the middle of her chest hanging to her knees. All the muscles, tendons, veins and everything else underneath her skin were visible where the cloth didn't cover, making her look like a walking corpse.

"A dragon!" the shaman exclaimed, clapping her hands. "I haven't had a dragon visit in more than twenty years!" She hobbled into the rain to stare up at Hiro. "Hiro, eh?" Hiro watched the floppy muscle on the back of her arm swing as she flourished a hand. "I am Sha Ogalala Karpoo Shampeder, but my friends call me Shampy." She squinted one eye at Hiro. "You can call me Sha Ogalala." After a moment of a stern glare she burst out laughing. "I'm just yanking your tail. You can call me Shampy. Everyone does!" She gawked at him as if he were the crazy one. "What are you doing in this rain?"

"We come with instructions from Rakgar of the Rock Cloud Ruck."

"We?" The faerie shifted to look past Hiro.

"My friend, Tog, and myself."

"Oh-ho!" she yelled, then frowned suddenly. "Two dragons! Well," she turned back to her home, "I've only room for one of you. One will have to stay outside in the rain."

"If you please, Sha," Hiro said as she scuttled away, "we must have your oath before we can proceed."

"My oath?" Shampy spun to leer at him. He noticed her blue cloth didn't have a drop of water on it. "Every faerie shares the oaths of dragons past. How dare you ask me to repeat one?!"

Long ago the faeries executed a spell to bind the tongues of every faerie unto death should they ever tell a human of the dragons' ability to speak. It had begun to be a sore spot with both species, as Hiro previously experienced.

"This is a personal issue," Hiro said before his temper could rise. "We have something to tell you that you must swear never to tell another soul. Will you so swear?"

"Perhaps you'll beg to Sha Ogalala after all," she hemmed. "Why should I swear anything to you?"

Hiro didn't back down. "Rakgar sends us. Are you his friend or not?"

"That depends." Shampy folded her arms over her chest. "I haven't been to the Rock Clouds in many years. Who is Rakgar these days?"

Many dragons knew the story of how the current Rakgar had gained his name and title. It happened at about the same time as Hiro's hatching. His father once gave him the strange memory of the current Rakgar, then named Freeg (for his friendship with the Rakgar in power, and others), suddenly fighting with the then-Rakgar. No one ever understood what happened between the friends to cause the discord. Young Freeg was a much larger and stronger dragon. The former Rakgar refused to step down after they disagreed. In the memory Hiro's father gave him, Freeg killed the former Rakgar quickly and took his place in succession.

Hiro intoned his leader's full name to summarize the story: "Rakgar feira Freeg Ido Havin."

"Ah, formerly Freeg and son of Havin," Shampy grinned. "I remember Havin. Mean as his name, that one.

His son is Rakgar, you say? He must have scared the previous Rakgar to death, he's so large. Why is it he sent you?"

"Something is attacking faeries and humans. He sent us to see if you could tell us anything about it," Hiro said.

Shampy looked between Tog and Hiro. "Does the oath have anything to do with your question?"

"Nothing whatsoever."

Shampy scowled without fear at the dragon in front of her. Somehow she even seemed taller than Hiro. "Then I swear I'll never reveal to anyone what you reveal to me."

"Give me your oath."

Shampy's jaw worked, but she stifled her frustration. "I give you my oath as a dragon gives his wyrd. May you strike me down if I should break it."

Hiro stared, but the faerie held his cold gaze. Finally Hiro turned to Tog. "Anna, come here."

The sodden princess stepped from behind Tog. Tog stood still, as if carved from the side of a mountain. One eye watched the woman, but the other stared hard at the faerie. Hiro wondered whether Tog was being protective or pleading for help.

Shampy sucked in a loud gasp when Anna came into view. "By Cozad!" the faerie used the god of curses' name. Her eyes widened and she pointed wordlessly at Anna, then turned the finger on Hiro. "You've spoken to her?" she asked.

Hiro nodded.

"But…" Shampy's gaze fell to her hand. She turned it over.

"No," Hiro said. He half-hoped the spell might have been broken as Kradik insisted it would be when he tortured Hiro for this result. But the cruel faerie shaman had been wrong. "The spell has not been lifted," he told Shampy.

Shampy's hand curled into a fist and she let it descend to her side. She sighed, "Go around to the back and we'll see what we can do."

When she disappeared into the hut, Hiro turned back to Tog. "She took it better than I expected."

"What did you expect?" Anna whispered.

Hiro avoided her eye. "I thought she might try to murder you for me."

11

TEARS

The two dragons slipped around to the back of the hut. Anna followed in silence. Hiro doubted there would be any space at all inside, let alone enough for a fully grown dragon. Turning the corner he saw a large opening covered only with a thick brown cloth. The cloth, like many others around the hut, remained dry despite the rain. Hiro glanced at his companions.

"Don't look at me," Tog grumbled, falling to the ground. Anna motioned Hiro toward the opening. She wouldn't want to be alone with the shaman for any amount of time. Hiro grit his teeth and pushed his head past the curtain. Anna removed the hide from around her and followed close behind.

The outside of the shaman's home seemed strange, but the inside seemed like another world. As they entered, Shampy lit several candles along the walls, illuminating things Hiro was certain could only be seen in this home. Totems hung from rafters joined by strange objects floating in jars of liquids. Few cloths crowded the space, but they were interspersed with plants and roots: some in jars, some out of jars, some growing out of jars, some growing out of the walls and floor. One section of the counter overflowed with containers of all shapes and sizes holding a variety of ingredients. There were sparkly powders, twisted brown root-like things, some dead bugs, some live bugs and shallow dishes most definitely made of dragon scales filled with small bones.

The variety of scents to assail him upon entering almost made Hiro black out. A strong musk odor came from strips of leather-like material stretched across wooden planks. He had to hold his breath entirely as he pushed past a pot of flowers that smelled of rotting meat. The most potent scent of tang came from a purple plant with feathers at the top. But beyond the sights and smells, most surprising of all was the fact that once Hiro squeezed through the opening, he found he could settle along one side of the room comfortably. By some majikal process the hut was far bigger on the inside.

Hiro noticed a small swirl of smoke hovering over a glossy black rock against the far wall. He stared, wondering if and when the smoke would dissipate. When Shampy noticed his gaze she walked over to it. Her picking up the black rock didn't disperse the smoke, either; it simply followed.

"Fascinating, isn't it?" Shampy brought the miniature tornado closer, but Hiro pulled away. "It was a gift from my former apprentice when he departed my service." She watched the smoke swirl, even brushing her hand through it, but nothing swayed the course of the current. "Kradik had a certain flare of originality." Shampy said this while focusing on the swirling smoke, so she missed the shared glance between Hiro and Anna. Hiro's scales rippled with a flush of anger.

"Kradik was your apprentice?" Anna asked, trying to keep her voice steady.

"Yes, and my nephew," Shampy said, setting the miniature smoke tornado aside again. "Do you know him?"

"I met him in Kingstor," Anna answered.

Hiro lurched to his feet. "Kradik is no friend to dragons." His fire burned at the memory of the agony beset on him by the faerie.

"Come now," Shampy's eyes widened, "all faeries are friends to dragons." She flicked her hand over her shoulder as if shooing a pest.

Hiro narrowed his eyes. "Your apprentice tortured me."

Shampy spread her hands. "I cannot be responsible for another's actions. Perhaps you misunderstood his position."

"I misunderstood nothing."

"Then a miscommunication." Before Hiro could reply she continued. "Whatever the case may be, I am a friend of your Rakgar and will serve you to the best of my ability." She steepled her fingertips and opened her mouth to speak. Hiro saw Anna flinch when the faerie jerked her head around to yell angry, unintelligible words over her shoulder. She didn't acknowledge their wide eyes when she turned back to her guests with a smile. "Now, you've come to ask about some sort of creature, is that right?"

Anna and Hiro shared an uneasy silence before Hiro decided to settle again to the floor. "A black creature attacking humans and some faeries," Hiro said.

Anna stood beside Hiro. "It appeared in the Courageous Kingdom, but seems to be moving toward Kingstor Noble. Do you know what it is and how to stop it?"

"Ah," Shampy held up a single gnarled finger, "but that is not the right question to ask first. The first question should be the matter of my payment." The muscle on Shampy's forehead lifted her eyebrows at the pair.

"Payment?" Hiro asked. "But I thought you would help us as a favor to Rakgar?"

Shampy nodded. "Yes, but even Rakgar knows I must eat, so my favors come at a price. The first favor was that I didn't already send you on your way."

Anna touched her neck and wrists although she must already know they were bare. "I have no gold," she stated.

"I have no need for gold, young lady," Shampy answered with unblinking eyes on the dragon. "All I need is ingredients."

"Where would we…?" Anna began, but noticed the two creatures scrutinizing each other. "Surely you can't think…"

"Dragons are the most majikal creatures in existence." Shampy's eyes wandered unabashed over Hiro. He could see her vessels dilate as her blood pumped harder on its course. "You come to me rich enough."

After a few moments, Hiro made a decision. "What did you have in mind?"

Shampy shrugged. "I'm a reasonable woman. I see you've lost one talon already. Would you be willing to part with another one, or the tip of your tail, perhaps?"

"You're mad," Anna whispered, eyes wide. She spun to face Hiro. "Surely you don't plan to negotiate?"

"We have no choice," he growled, and locked eyes with the faerie. "I'll give you no claw or tail, but I have more to offer."

"Yes," Shampy smiled, "like tears."

"Tears?" Hiro shook his head. "Dragons don't cry."

"Ah, but they do," Shampy nodded. "Every creature weeps—well, except a banshee—but dragons cry more than any of you would ever admit."

Hiro shook his head again. "What about scales? Or fire?"

"Dragon fire?" Shampy spun in a circle and kicked a nearby wall, but abruptly met Hiro's eye as sharp as ever. "I can get dragon fire cheap from anyone!"

"Scales, then."

"Scales are also easy to get. They're the only bit of a dragon that falls off and doesn't turn to ash." Shampy rummaged through some bottles. She pulled out a small, round glass orb with a circle cut into the top. "But the tears are the most valuable and are most necessary for this majik."

"Why?" Anna and Hiro asked at the same time.

Shampy narrowed her eyes at Anna but turned to answer Hiro. "This," she indicated the orb, "is made majikally from the crystal formed in the Longhorn Mountains on the other side of Avonoa. When filled with dragon tears, it will seal seamlessly. To look through a dragon's eye is to see into the past, present or future. Since we can't look through a dragon's eye, we must use their tears.

"As you indicated, dragons don't cry readily, making this the most difficult of ingredients to find. Difficult—not impossible. The Longhorn Mountains are named so because of the Long-horned Trolls who protect it, so the crystal isn't without its own perils to obtain as well. Hence, very few of these majikal orbs exist in the world." She tipped the container into Anna's hands, who handled it with awe. "Without dragon tears, I can't fill this crystal ball. Without your tears, I cannot give you the answers you seek."

Anna and Hiro shared another glance. Hiro was sure there had to be another way, but he knew he wouldn't get it out of this faerie. "I'm sure some dragons might be able to, but I certainly can't cry on demand," he said.

Shampy sighed. She shuffled to the opposite side of Hiro, away from Anna. Hiro saw the flash of metal from the corner of his eye. He caught sight of a blade glittering with the same multi-colored shimmer on the edge as the one Kradik had used to remove his talon. He roared as it plunged into his claw.

With surprising agility for one so stooped, Shampy swung away from his roaring maw while keeping the blade in place. "Contain your rage, dragon!" Shampy shouted. "Bottled emotion is the best way to force yourself to cry! Try to think of something incredibly sad."

"What are you doing?" Anna screamed. She fumbled to put the crystal ball aside and help Hiro at the same time, but the faerie forestalled her.

"Hold onto that, my dear. Else how will you catch the tears we need? Tears are necessary for the majik to be performed." Turning back to Hiro, she grumbled, "You said yourself that you can't cry on demand, so I created the next best option." Shampy grinned, twisting the blade deeper into Hiro's claw.

Hiro endeavored to contain his fire while the blade sliced deeper and deeper. He struggled against wanting to mangle the old faerie. He groaned and his leg shook. Shampy began pummeling the hilt of the knife with her fist. Hiro groaned louder.

"What's going on in here?" Tog bellowed, pushing his head through the curtain. "What do you think you're doing?" he yelled at Shampy.

"No room for you!" she yelled over her shoulder at him. "Wait outside!"

Anna's eyes twitched between the three beings, but rested more often on Hiro. Her hands shifted as if wanting to abandon the crystal orb.

Through clenched teeth, Hiro moaned, "I'll explain later," and shoved Tog's head out of the curtain again with his hind leg.

It felt to Hiro like Kradik was cutting off his talon all over again—with a dry stick. Pain cut along the edge of all his talons and sank deep within his claw. Icy pain climbed his limb. He ground his teeth together and looked to see Anna doing the same. Frigid pain pulsed up his limb over and over, but he could withstand it. "You'll have to do more than needle me to make me cry, witch," he growled.

"I can't do more without taking off a limb," Shampy worked the blade back and forth. The muscles and tendons in her hand palpitated as she delved into similar muscles of Hiro's. After a moment she stopped and added, "Unless...."

"What?" Anna yelled in frustration when the faerie's voice faded away.

Hiro reminded himself that the pain was necessary for tears—and tears were necessary for answers—when he heard the clatter of tools behind him, then grinding. He closed his eyes as his head quaked from the pain. His claw vibrated. It felt as if the faerie were twisting it off by hand! His heart pounded. His fire burned hotter than a demon. He couldn't feel the rest of his body. Only the pain in his claw existed.

He pried his eyes open. Anna hovered in his vision with fear and worry on her face, so he snapped them shut again. It was bad enough that she knew dragons could talk, but now she would be able to tell everyone she had seen a dragon cry.

Hiro thought of his father. He decided to dwell on his father's death to force a tear from his eye. He missed his father terribly these past few months, but had never once shed a tear. After all, death was another step in life. He knew his father, alongside his mother, watched him from the World of Souls. He couldn't truckle to sorrow over the thought.

Hiro shut out the thought of the human watching him in terror. He reached into his mind for memories of his father and mother. He didn't want to show weakness, but with this thought, his mind struck on something: a memory his father gave him long ago.

Tusten's own father, Horoskin, had been teaching him. Hiro recalled the memory with perfect clarity as if it had happened to him only yesterday. "Never show weakness to an enemy or anyone else. But remember that meekness is not weak. Meekness is allowing yourself to submit for the benefit of good. It takes a strong will to submit so fully."

Meekness, Hiro told himself. *Anna will not see my weakness.*

He opened his eye to see her blank mask of anger standing before him. She hated the faerie enough for both of them. Water flowed silently down her cheeks, so Hiro fed his emotions from it. He gathered all the pain and frustration, anger and suffering into his eyes. Instantly they swam with warm, wet tears. Before he could rejoice that the tears had begun to flow, he saw images in them. Shocking, terrifying images. Things he couldn't believe would happen.

Hiro used the visions to feed the flow of tears, pressing all his confusion, anger and pain away from his heart and into his eyes. Beyond the images, he could see Anna's jaw drop open. She shifted her fingers only slightly on the ball in order to collect the precious water. As each tear fell, the visions changed.

Hiro saw himself facing Tog, but Tog bared his fangs and whipped away from him in obvious disgust. Drip. He saw Rakgar strike down Prakyndar to kill him. Drip. Milah bowed his head in acquiescence to Hiro. Drip. Priya flew out of a burning mountain with what appeared to be a bundle dressed like Anna in her claw.

Drip. Milah, Mitashio and Prak lying broken and bleeding on the edge of death. Drip. Visi bleeding with a gaping wound in her chest. She reached out to Hiro with the last flicker of her fire. Drip. A man with hair as black as Hiro's scales. Hiro didn't know him, but he seemed familiar. He was dirty and bleeding and chained to a stone wall. Drip. Anna. In the Rock Clouds. Standing naked in the open before Rakgar and dozens more dragons as well. Rakgar. With pure rage in his eye, lifted a claw to end her. Drip.

The images faded along with the pain and tears. Hiro was vaguely aware of Anna yelling at Shampy to stop, indicating the full and sealed crystal ball. She set the ball on a counter and turned back to Hiro, placing her hands on his snout.

Hiro could hear moaning. "Are you all right?" Anna asked him through the sound. Her hands and chin shook.

He swallowed before he could answer and the noise stopped. He realized he must have been making the sound. He swallowed again, but couldn't trust his voice. The visions he had seen, the pain and emotions he had experienced acted like rough tree bark scraping against his throat. He nodded and laid his head on the stone floor.

Anna pursed her lips and pushed his snout away to confront the faerie. "What did you do to him?"

"What needed to be done," Shampy muttered back, hunched over her jars.

"Torture? You had to torture him?" Anna growled. She sounded very much like Priya in that moment.

For the first time, Shampy seriously considered Anna. "You're a fiery young thing. I see why you can handle a dragon." She nodded when Anna seemed taken aback, but waved toward Hiro. "He said himself it wasn't enough."

"Well?" Tog shoved his head through the curtain again.

Anna punched her fists on her hips, still glaring at Shampy. "It's done," she answered.

"And a great job of it, too!" Shampy held aloft two small jars of a thick silvery liquid. "I was just going to take a little blood, but I got some marrow from the bargain, too, thanks to a stubborn dragon." She flashed a grim half-smile, placing the small jars next to four larger ones filled with dark red blood.

"Marrow?" Anna queried, studying the smaller jars.

"Oh yes," Shampy nodded. She wiped her hands on the bottom of the dirty blue cloth she wore then turned to rifle through a cabinet. "Taking marrow is extremely painful for any creature, but especially for dragons, because everything is majikally entwined."

"It couldn't be all that bad if Hiro managed it," Tog said, watching his friend.

"Tog," Hiro gurgled from the floor, "next time I'll allow you to take my place and you can tell me what you think. I promise."

"Don't make promises you don't intend to keep," Tog said.

Shampy pushed past him. "Oh, flutterish nonsense. He'll be fine, of course." The faerie held out a round flarote bulb. "Eat this." She shoved it into Hiro's mouth. "You'll be good as a summer cloud in no time."

"How can you know that?" Anna asked. She watched Hiro a little too closely for his comfort.

"Everyone knows that!" Shampy snapped.

The flarote burned through Hiro and immediately healed his aching claw. The pain deep inside his bone disappeared as warmth spread throughout him. His heart beat faster and his fire burned hotter. Tog stared at Hiro meaningfully as the cut along the top of his claw healed instantly, leaving no trace of the torment he'd just experienced.

Flarote was a wonderful herb. A little mushroom grown only in warm, dark places, it resembled a fat little fire frozen in time. Everyone knew flarote healed animals of all shapes and sizes, but it had an accelerated and drastic effect on dragons. If dragons ate too much flarote, it would kill them. This information they guarded from every creature. Now Hiro felt he would have to do more to dissuade Anna and Shampy from knowing the truth.

"Your claw," Anna pointed in shock. "It's completely healed."

She assessed Hiro. "I'll be fine," he told her. "It must have healed the surface, but it still aches deep inside. I just need to rest." It was a lie, of course. He could have flown circles that moment.

"Would you like more flarote?" Shampy asked.

"No," Hiro answered, maybe a little too quickly. When Shampy and Anna furrowed their brows in concern, he said, "I would hate to be forced to re-supply you, as well." Shampy shrugged her shoulders, unconcerned, but Anna peered at Hiro. "I'll be fine," he insisted again. "Let's just get our answers and get out of here."

12

FAVORS

With her precious payment safely stored away, Shampy pulled a small table and two chairs out from a wall nearby. Tog stayed behind the curtain but kept his head peeking through. Hiro sensed he didn't like being left out. Shampy offered one chair to Anna before seating herself across from her. The crystal ball, now resting in a pile of dried leaves, sat between them. Anna leaned in close to the leaves to sniff. "Mint?" she questioned Shampy.

"Mint is good for dragons' eyes," she said. Seeing the grin on Hiro's face she added, "And most dragons love it."

When Anna's eyes popped to Hiro, he shrugged, "It's the only plant worth eating, anyway."

Shampy shushed them, but as soon as she opened her mouth to speak she snapped it shut again. Rolling her head toward the dark portion of her home she hollered,

"Can't you see I'm busy?" She shook her head, muttering something about invisible kangaroos, and began again. Hiro wondered if his expression mirrored Anna's apparent confusion.

Staring into the ball, Shampy muttered words in Faerie tongue under her breath, slurring the sounds together. Faster and faster the words flowed. As she intoned, she swayed slightly in rhythm and her hands danced over the ball. When her voice stopped, she focused into its depths.

"The creature you seek—" she whispered, narrowing her eyes. Rain trickled against the thatched roof. "—is an Earth Wraith."

"A wraith?" Anna whispered.

"To conjure an Earth Wraith is dark majik indeed," Shampy continued. "Wraiths are difficult to control. Even those who practice dark majik are afraid to conjure a wraith. Once created, they can easily turn and destroy the conjurer then lay waste to everything and everyone they hold dear. Wraiths can be exorcised from any element: earth, water, fire or air. This one has been brought from the earth and must be sent back to the earth. It's drawn to warm salt water. It feeds at night on moisture extracted from either animal or human. Unchecked, it could consume this entire world."

"An Earth Wraith…" Anna whispered again, "but who conjured it? And why?"

Shampy muttered again in a low voice. As she watched the ball her face slackened into a blank stare. Finally her grim eyes met Anna's. "The centaurs."

Anna's and Tog's wide eyes shot to Hiro, as his stomach dropped and his neck stiffened upright. "Was it done with Joss's consent?" Hiro asked the shaman.

She squinted into the ball, then looked up at Hiro. "Who's Joss?"

Hiro shook his head. "Never mind."

Shampy murmured a few more words. "You'll find the creature in the village of Eoaa, on the west side of the Torthoth Mountains. A day north of the mountain border village of Yiksee."

"I know that village," Anna told Hiro. "I can lead you there."

Shampy muttered some more incomprehensible words, stared into the ball again, then dropped her eyes. "I can't see what will happen should you choose to confront it."

The faerie, dragon and human all backed away from their hovering stances over the crystal ball. "What must we do?" Hiro asked.

"It will return to the ground to sleep during the day and only travel far enough to find food at night, so you should easily be able to catch up to it. An Earth Wraith is drawn to warm salt water, but it's repelled by dragon fire," she said, then stood to rummage through her piles of dragon scale dishes. "I'm sure you'll find the creature where large amounts of people or animals gather." She abandoned the dishes to pull a jar with feathers and a multi-colored snake-like creature from a cabinet. "The more concentrated the amount, the more it will draw in the wraith. Or the warmer the water, the more draw it will have as well." Her voice echoed as if she was in a cavern when she stuffed the upper half of her body into the cabinet.

"Yes, but how do we destroy it?" Anna asked, trying not to stare at Shampy's hind end wiggling from the opening.

"In a moment!" Shampy waggled a finger in the air behind her. Once she extricated herself from the cabinet, she shuffled to the same wall she had kicked earlier and kicked it again (but this time she hurt her foot) before she ducked under the table. Hiro noticed a small dent in the wall. It must offend her often. "Oh, yes!" she exclaimed to the bottom of the seemingly empty table.

Standing up again took her considerably longer than expected, but eventually Shampy brushed small blue feathers and gold dust from a black box at the back of the counter. She applied one feather to the top of her head, where it disappeared. She lifted the box lid only enough to slip her gnarled fingers inside, feel around the box, and suddenly jerk her hand out. The lid clattered and the box seemed to right itself. She opened her hand to produce a small roll of something that looked like brown ribbon. She unraveled a section of it for display. "This must be wrapped around the wraith, then you must burn the wraith and the ribbon with dragon fire."

Anna held her hand out to inspect the roll. "What is it made of?"

Shampy's wicked grin reappeared. She rolled the ribbon, pursed her lips, and shook her head. "Better you don't ask, my dear."

Anna proffered the ribbon to Hiro, but he nodded to her. "Hold onto it," he said, and she tucked it into a pocket of her tattered dress.

"Be careful," Shampy warned Hiro. "Although dragons haven't much moisture in them, you still have some, and plenty of warmth. An Earth Wraith can kill a dragon just as easily as it can kill a human."

———

The trio gave their thanks to the faerie and took their leave. Shampy offered Anna a place to sleep inside the hut, but Anna politely refused. Instead, she joined the dragons away from the shaman's home to sleep among the trees under the damp lydik hide. Curling up next to Hiro in the misty rain, she pulled the roll of ribbon from her pocket.

"It feels soft," she told the dragons, "and familiar somehow." She continued to run her hands over it. "Almost like silk, but not any silk I've ever felt." She cast her eyes up to Hiro. "And I've felt quite a few."

"Perhaps it's from a distant land," Hiro said.

"Or it's the silk of some disgusting ancient worm," Tog suggested. "Maybe Shampy was protecting your delicate ears from the gory details of gathering it."

"She had no qualms with sharing the details of the wraith," she said back. "Why would she try to protect me from this?" She rerolled the ribbon and put it away. "I don't know," she said, snugging her hide around her again. "I don't trust her."

"Rakgar trusts her," Tog said.

"Do you trust Rakgar?" she said to Tog, but the question was directed at both dragons.

"With our lives," Hiro answered her.

She nodded. "That's good. Because it might be your lives that you give."

"Rakgar's judgment isn't what bothers me," Hiro told her. "Anyone can be deceived. But what I can't believe is that the centaurs would conjure this creature."

"Why not?" Anna asked. "Centaurs have majishuns just like every other civilization."

"Yes," Tog said, "but they're not nearly as practiced as the faeries."

"Nor do they dwell on dark majik as much," Hiro finished. "I'm friends with centaurs. They wouldn't do something like this."

"Then perhaps Shampy is lying," Anna said.

Hiro glared toward the little shaman hut. "That's what I'm afraid of."

"Well," Anna leaned back against Hiro's warm belly, "we'll know if she's lying when we get to Eoaa."

"We?" Hiro said.

Anna sat up to look at him. "Yes, 'we.' Don't think you're leaving me here with that mad cat."

"I was thinking we'd take you closer to Kingstor, actually."

Anna leaned in next to his face. "I'm coming with you," she said firmly. "I know how to get to Yiksee." She leaned back against his ribs again. "And I can't just pass you the memory of how to get there."

"You asked for that one," Tog said, resting his head on the ground.

"It will be too dangerous," Hiro told her, "and you'll slow us down."

"I'm coming with you," she insisted. "How do you think you'll use this?" She shook her fist with the ribbon tucked inside. "How would it look for two dragons to deal with this on their own? Any human who sees you will think they've lost their mind!"

"As much as I hate these words on my tongue," Tog muttered, licking his fangs for effect, "the human is right."

Hiro turned a wary eye on his friend. "Whose side are you on?"

Tog raised his head. "She chose to come with us in the first place and we can't do much without her."

"Exactly," Anna said.

"Snap it, human," Tog gnarred at her. "We don't have to worry about the danger yet, anyway. All we're doing is looking for answers. We know what we're dealing with. We know what needs to be done. Once we see the creature for ourselves, we can take the information back to Rakgar to learn what he would have us do with it."

"What?!" Anna yelled. "You're not going to help me kill this thing?!"

"Why should we?" Tog snapped back at her. "We didn't conjure it. It doesn't threaten us. Only HUMANS do!!"

Anna turned an angry eye on Hiro. "You can't agree with this drivel?"

Hiro's eyes bounced between his friend and the human. Finally, he looked directly at Anna. "You saved my life," he told her. "I'll always be indebted to you. That's why I'm allowing you to come along. We'll get all the information we need, but…" He sighed and forced his heart to soften against her. "Tog is right. Our duty is to find out what this thing is and how it affects the dragons, then take the information back to Rakgar so he can make a decision as to what should be done."

Anna shook her head slowly. "Who would ever think that dragons were such cowards?"

13

REND

"Fly north," Anna pointed.

"I *am* flying north," Hiro grunted back.

"You're going too far west."

"You said northwest."

"Yes, I said northwest, not west."

"I'm flying northwest."

"No, you're flying too far west."

"I am not!"

"You are, too!"

"I don't want to fly too close to Yiksee."

"But you have to stay on course."

"I am on course!"

"No, you're too far west!"

"I'm going around the storm."

"Now you're afraid of a little rain?"

"I thought it would be more comfortable for you."

"Oh, now you're concerned for me, are you?"

"Not anymore!"

"SNAP IT!" Tog yelled. "BOTH OF YOU! You bicker like my grand-sires!" Anna and Hiro gaped at him.

The trio had been flying for a day and a half. For all that time, Anna had managed to remain still with the lydik hide wrapped around her as best she could. A steady drizzle of rain kept the flying constant as well. They stopped to rest whenever Anna began to fall asleep in Hiro's claw, yet Anna never once asked to be set down. Hiro had a funny feeling she knew just how much she would put up with.

"But he's going—" Anna started, but clamped her jaw shut when she received a dangerous glance from Tog's eye.

Tog lowered his voice. "We can't be so loud, so close to the humans."

"I've been to Yiksee before," Anna told him, keeping her voice low. "They don't have much of a garrison. Just a few guards to keep the peace and a lieutenant to manage them."

"We'll skirt the village and fly for Eoaa," Hiro told them. Ignoring Anna's gaze, he caught a draft to deviate further north. Unfortunately, it also brought him down. The turbulence of flying through the rain buffeted the group, but Hiro sustained a tight hold on Anna's small form.

They flew past the last of the mountains of the Torthoth Range until the small border village came into view. Anna pointed through the rain-spattered surroundings. "There," she said, "you see? It's no more than a few homes. Yiksee is hardly a threat."

Sure enough, the place she pointed out displayed a handful of roofs from which wisps of smoke rose to be smothered by the heavy clouds overhead. Hiro turned to Tog, who gave a little shrug of his shoulders. "Still," Tog said, "we should—"

Tog's statement cut short when an arrow buzzed by, slicing his leg. Anna gasped, but wisely said nothing. All three of them looked into the trees below as three more arrows hurtled toward them. Hiro jounced Anna, but the dragons avoided the arrows once they saw their trajectory.

Tog flew in front of Hiro and the two dragons' eyes met. Hiro jerked his chin at Tog, motioning to give him the lead. Without a word, Tog dropped his left wing to aim away from the attackers toward the west. They flew toward the top of a flat-faced cliff as more arrows whistled behind them.

Finally beyond the arrows range, Tog reached the rocky ledge first. Before Hiro could set down, he steadied himself in the air. Since he couldn't land on all fours, he back-drafted to put his hind legs down first. Anna clung silently to his front leg. As he exposed his belly, a new hail of arrows sprayed at them—this time from the trees in front of them. Both Hiro and Tog let out roars as two dragon-killer bolts burrowed into Tog and three found their marks in Hiro.

Tog roared and ran down the mountain along the cliff edge, but Hiro took the shortest route down by careening down the cliff backward. With arrows pouring around him, Hiro dared not open his wings. Instead, he pulled Anna into his chest, curling his body around her and hoping the lydik hide would help cushion her as well. Falling at the bottom would be painful for him, but he knew it would be deadly for the human.

Hiro had experienced this falling sensation when he left the Rock Clouds with Visi's help the first time. In that escape, Visi also bestowed the gift of allowing him to feel the pounding force of being smashed by rock, but it didn't make either experience any less painful. Hiro's roar echoed off the mountain walls when he hit the bottom. His scales cracked against rock, sapping his strength. He crumpled on the ground, but fastened around Anna. A slight incline at the bottom rolled the pair into a dark cavern at the base of the cliff.

Hiro groaned as he peeled his wings and legs away from Anna. She flung the hide and her other supplies to the ground. She was unharmed. "Are you alright?" she whispered to the dragon.

Hiro nodded and thumped his head on the ground. "Get the arrows out," he whispered back.

Two of the arrow shafts had broken off in the fall, but one remained intact. Anna pulled the longest one out first. Hiro let out a soft moan and she moved on to the next one.

"I'm sorry," Anna whispered again, wrapping her fingers around the next arrow. "This might hurt."

Before she could pull it out, Hiro held up a claw to her. "Quiet." Anna stopped moving. He was surprised when she didn't scurry to the opening of the shallow cave to peer out. She didn't even question Hiro, which impressed him further. He lifted his head and brought it up next to her. He faced the sheet of rain. "Someone's coming," he breathed, so low that only she would hear.

"Tog?" she whispered back. She closed her eyes when he shook his head.

Hiro gently wrapped his claws around Anna's waist, lifted her from his belly and placed her on the rocky floor between him and the back wall of the cave. "Don't move."

"Wait," she whispered, barely breathing. "Perhaps I could talk to them. Reason with them."

"Yes, and explain why you're traveling in relative safety with two dragons," Hiro chided.

Anna's mouth dropped open, as if she was about to argue, but she snapped it shut. He turned back to face the entrance only a few claw lengths from them. He settled himself in front of her in a defensive posture and stared out the opening for the first sign of an attacker.

As he watched the pouring rain, Anna's breathing stopped. Hiro knew humans couldn't go without air for long, so a moment later he tilted his head to check on her. His own breath stopped and his stomach lurched. He spun around bodily when he saw the empty stone wall where she had been.

14

OBLITERATION

"I don't like it," Torgon grumbled at Philip's side. "The king should not be summoned by his own guests." He and Philip marched along the dark castle corridors toward the faeries' chambers. The rain pouring against the windows didn't do anything to help lighten Torgon's foul mood.

Torgon had heard the summons before heading to a promotion ceremony, so he'd donned his finest cloak to finish off his already impressively gilded outfit. Better to intimidate the faeries, or so he'd told Philip. Philip, however, had been poring over reports with his clerks. Taking Torgon's suggestion, he had also added an intricately embroidered coat to his casual silk shirt.

Philip shrugged, "Perhaps culturally, this is common for them."

"How so?" his general shot back. "Faeries don't have kings."

"Exactly. They wouldn't know the etiquette for seeking an audience."

"It's common courtesy among most cultures to seek out the person with whom you wish to speak, not make them come to you," he answered.

Philip stopped in the middle of the hallway. "What are you saying?"

Torgon spun to face him. Philip appreciated when his friend and general gave him his honest opinion. Like now. "They're trying to dictate your actions. Showing you that they're in control." He shook his head. "I think you should've insisted they come to you."

Philip nodded. "You might be right, but we still need to see what they want. You can say 'I told you so' later." He resumed his brisk pace down the hall.

Upon reaching the faeries' quarters, one of the four guards surrounding the pair of men knocked on the door.

"Come in," Qialla's voice called.

The guard opened the door, but Torgon put a hand in front of Philip. "At least allow me to go first," he said quietly. Philip waved for him to proceed before instructing the guards to remain outside unless called.

The stifling heat in the faeries' rooms almost knocked Philip over. He immediately regretted the fancy coat he'd put on last. Four enormous fires burned under cauldrons in the front chamber alone. Delicate tripod frames, saucers, bowls, phials and jars of all shapes and sizes congested tables, chairs and even corners of the floor. The windows all hung open with more instruments and herbs dripping over the ledges.

"Welcome, Your Majesty," Qialla said with a deep bow to Philip. The faeries still wore their cloaks and gloves, but hadn't donned the face covering. They kept their chins angled down. "I apologize for the breech in etiquette, but it was necessary for you to see the work we're doing."

"It's quite alright," Philip said with a brief glance at Torgon. "I'm glad to inspect your progress."

The two men ambled further into the room to observe the many wonders the faeries had to show them. "Please don't touch anything," Qialla added when Torgon extended a curious hand. "Many of these substances are delicate and a few are rather dangerous."

Qialla picked up a bowl with a thick, black substance oozing in it. "This," he said with reverence, "is what we've been researching." He picked up the point of a broken arrowhead and scraped it along the bottom of the bowl, scarcely covering the sharp tip. "All our tests show it should bring instant death to any dragon it punctures. We need only test it on a live one."

"Test it?" Torgon laughed. "And how do you propose we do that?"

"The same way you gathered much of the dragon ash we needed," he answered. "Set a trap."

"I thought you said the dragons were too smart to fall for the same trap twice."

Qialla had been addressing Philip, but now he turned to Torgon. "We needn't test it on the many," he said, then turned back to Philip. "You know the path of the black dragon. You could meet it before it ever reaches Kingstor Noble. With this." He held the arrow tip up for Philip to see the black coating over its sharp head.

"What can it do?" Philip asked.

"If you'll permit me," Qialla said. He set down the bowl with the remains of the dragon poison and picked up an empty, shallow dish no larger than his palm. Turning it over, Philip could see a shining yellow-orange hue and realized it wasn't a dish at all, but a dragon scale. Under this, he placed a few centimeters of a purplish rope-like material.

"As you know, when a dragon dies it turns to ash. This before you is part of a dragon's vein, majikally preserved from the ash state for these tests," Qialla told them. He tapped the blackened arrow against the scale. "If the arrow cannot pierce the scales, it has no effect. The same is true if it cannot puncture the hide. Unfortunately, our early tests have shown that the poison must be introduced to the dragon's anatomy through the blood stream." He scraped the arrow against the scale to demonstrate no change. "But once it penetrates the scales and hide—by any means that might make a dragon bleed—" he moved the scale out of the way to lightly press the arrow against the vein. With the least amount of pressure possible, the vein disappeared in a wisp of smoke, leaving behind a small pile of dragon ash.

Philip stared at the ash in shock. After a moment, Torgon asked, "Is it dangerous for humans to use?"

Qialla answered with a brisk, "You don't go around shooting each other with arrows, do you?"

"Accidents happen," Torgon stated. To Philip it sounded more like a threat.

Qialla's dark cowl shifted to Philip again. "May I remove my glove?"

Slightly confused why Qialla would ask permission, Philip blinked. "Of course."

Qialla nodded and pushed back his sleeve to slip off the heavy glove he wore. Humans were raised with tales of the faeries' skin being so hideous that they hid it from everyone. But Philip knew from his own tutors and recent experience that the faeries' skin was actually transparent, so they kept themselves hidden from humans. Whether that was for the humans' comfort or their own pride, no one could say. Philip had only seen Kradik's skin when he'd been splashed by the black dragon's blood. He couldn't speak for all of his men, but most of those present had averted their eyes almost immediately. However, the brief glimpse hung in his mind.

With the glove removed, Qialla worked his fingers. Philip watched, riveted at the marvel of the tendons, muscles, and veins shifting with the movement—pulling and pushing as they contracted and relaxed. Philip caught himself staring and wrenched his eyes into Qialla's cowl with what he hoped was an expectant look.

Once he had the men's attention, Qialla placed the same blackened arrow tip used on the dragon vein against the back of his own wrist. He ripped the arrow tip across his wrist with his other, still-gloved, hand.

Philip and Torgon leaned closer as the arrow fell away. Red blood pulsed from the veins he severed with the movement, but only for a second. As they watched, the muscles and one of the tendons grew together, sealing themselves seamlessly. Within two blinks, Qialla's wrist was whole again and unblemished except for the few drops of blood that had seeped from the wound.

"Incredible," Philip whispered.

"Too good to be true," Torgon grunted. When Qialla's and Philip's gazes met his, Torgon's brow set in a fierce line aimed at the faerie.

"Torgon," Philip tried to chasten his general.

But Torgon's eyes never left Qialla. "We both know faerie anatomy may look similar to humans', but there are many differences—some of which might protect the faeries better than humans." He began to remove his own glove, but Philip placed his hand over it.

"Torgon," he tried to caution again, "is this really necessary?"

Without pause, Torgon held out his naked wrist for the faerie. "I want to make sure my men will be safe."

"Of course," Qialla answered. Philip knew he wasn't imagining the smile in the faerie's voice. The arrow point slashed Torgon's wrist in one fluid movement. Torgon didn't flinch.

Finally, Torgon's curiosity overcame his mistrust. His eyes wavered to his hand as the skin pulled together, somewhat slower than the faerie's, but whole again nonetheless.

"Are you satisfied, General?" Qialla asked.

Torgon pulled a cloth from his pocket to dab the blood away. "For now."

"It's impressive," Philip repeated, attempting to soothe the situation. "How soon can I equip my men with those arrows?" In the back of his mind he laid plans to fill his own quiver first.

"Unfortunately," Qialla motioned toward the scant remains in the bowl, "this is all we have for now. As you can tell, the substance must be kept at a certain temperature until it is applied to the arrow points. Plus, it's extremely time-consuming to make. We don't have the resources to make large amounts of it here in the castle. Especially at this time of year."

"What needs to be done?" Torgon asked.

"Kradik and I will travel with the company of men you assigned to us, in search of a location to produce and distribute the poison. As I've told you in the past, flarote grows abundantly in the Great Northern Mountain. Kradik and I have considered the possibility of setting up production within the mountain itself and establishing a halfway point between there and Kingstor where the finished product could be distributed easily."

Philip nodded. "Very well. We'll leave you to your work. Please let us know what you'll need for the journey and how soon."

Moments later, Qialla nodded them out of the smoldering room. Once the door closed behind them, Torgon stopped in his tracks to stare out the window across the hallway as rain trickled down against it.

Philip stopped next to him. "Speak your mind."

Torgon sighed. "I was just wondering if the gods have a special punishment for xenocide."

15

MINISCULE CAPTORS

Hiro stared at the empty brown-and-gray-streaked rock face behind him. No seams or fissures of any kind appeared. Anna had disappeared without a trace and with nowhere to go. Confused and frustrated, Hiro slapped a claw against the rock wall. "Anna?" he whispered.

Nothing.

He opened his mouth to call her again, but heard footsteps crunch outside the cave. He momentarily forgot the woman when he saw shadows of three humans with arrows nocked on bows. They blundered closer to the cave, but didn't appear to spot Hiro.

Suddenly, his vision blurred and went black. It seemed like his eyes were closed, but he knew they were open. He felt a force pulling him backward into the rock wall, only the wall didn't stop his movement. Not sure what to expect, he swung his body to attempt a blind and silent attack.

Upon turning, his eyes widened in horror. The darkness lifted beyond where the wall should have been, with little glowing rocks illuminating the cavern from the ceiling. Anna knelt on the ground with a cloth gag around her head, covering her mouth. Her hands and arms, compressed behind her, must have been tied. Her chest heaved as if she'd been struggling, but she sat cowed by the strangest being Hiro had ever seen.

The creature had the pointed ears of a faerie, the large eyes of a centaur and mottled gray skin decorated with curving blue lines on his hands, neck and sides of his face. Had they both been standing, he would have reached only as high as Anna's middle. Anna twitched her shoulders, but the little man's small hands must have been stronger than their size belied, because she could barely move.

In the dank surroundings of the cave the creature's bright-colored clothes stood out in abstract. A fitted red tunic sculpted well-worked muscles on his short arms and a bright blue sash with strange symbols embroidered in brilliant yellow crossed an intimidating chest. Copious bejeweled knives encircled his slim waist and ankles. Around his forehead he wore a silver circlet with multi-colored gems, all the same shape and size, equidistant apart and organized as if they served a purpose beyond just decoration. The circlet held down locks of orange hair with blood-red tips hanging next to his chin.

Two more of these gray-skin creatures, similarly sashed but with different shades of clothing underneath, had short green and blue hair. They held small swords, the size of one of Hiro's talons, pointed toward Anna. The one with green hair trained his eye on her, never wavering when a fully grown dragon emerged through a stone wall. The other, with blue hair and a streak of purple on the side, held the sword pointed at Anna's throat, but glared at Hiro. Message received.

Hiro dared his eyes to search the remainder of the space. Three more of these gray-skins held swords pointed at Hiro. Two of them, with yellow hair brighter than Anna's, had half the number of gems in their circlets as the one restraining Anna. The last gray-skin Hiro saw, who looked to be female from her softer features encompassed by sharply angled blood-red hair, caught Hiro's eye. Once she held his gaze, she placed a finger to her lips. Keeping her sword pointed at Hiro, she stepped silently to the wall and touched her hand to it.

Nothing seemed to happen from the touch, but as the red-haired creature removed her hand, she looked up with confidence at what should have been an imposing figure of a dragon. "I am Shvika. You, dragon, and your human companion are prisoners of the goblins." The word "prisoners" seemed to echo off the cavern walls.

Hiro couldn't take this behavior. Despite the pain caused by the arrows still buried in his belly, he lowered his head and snarled at the little gray-skin named Shvika, but still she didn't waver.

"Do not test me, dragon. My guards will not hesitate to kill your human if you try anything. We've slaughtered humans for less than such." She narrowed one eye at him. "Even the lowest of goblins is more powerful than you could possibly imagine."

Hiro laughed in his mind. *This tiny creature is threatening a dragon?* he thought.

"I make no threats, dragon," she said, slipping her sword into her belt. Faster than Hiro thought possible, Shvika sprang forward to make contact with Hiro's claw. A shock like a bolt of lightning shook Hiro's frame. His knees buckled and he fell to the ground on his side, narrowly avoiding further embedding the two arrows still protruding from his middle. Hiro caught his breath as he lay on the floor of the cavern, but Shvika wasn't done. With the arrows within reach she stepped forward and yanked them free.

The arrows clattered to the floor and she indicated the two yellow-hairs. "Mlika, Morkni, take the rear. Schvek, Thrask, resume guard. Keeahrspi," she indicated the orange-haired fellow restraining Anna, "the gag is no longer necessary."

After feeling Shvika's shock, Hiro realized they had no choice. He watched the well-sculpted Keeahrspi untie the gag from Anna and lift her to her feet. He drew his sword to force her steps, but it was unnecessary. Hiro wondered if the little man would have treated her more gently if he'd known her name. Probably not. The look in his eye said the treatment was as much as they might expect—if not worse.

They left the blue- and green-haired goblins at the solid wall. Before they were out of sight, Hiro saw them turn to stare at the wall. He thought it odd until the blue-hair pointed to a random spot on the wall and the green-hair nodded. What did they see?

Letting his gaze shift from the goblins they'd left behind, Hiro limped down the tunnel, following Shvika. He saw more tunnels leading off in different directions. Snaking lines sparkled in miniscule rivulets through the rocks. He caught the distinct sound of hammers, large and small, down one of the side tunnels.

"What is this place?" Anna asked as she shuffled along in Keeahrspi's grip. "Is it a mine?"

"This is our home," Shvika said, "and this is what we do."

"Kidnap innocents that accidentally trespass?" Anna said.

All the goblins stopped at the same time. Anna actually wrenched her arm and fell backwards into Keeahrspi. "No human is innocent!" he bellowed as she tumbled to the floor.

Shvika held up her hand to forestall him. "If I were you, I would allow the dragon to voice questions."

When Anna recovered enough to meet Shvika's eyes, she asked, "What makes you think a dragon can talk?"

The goblins all laughed mirthlessly and Keeahrspi hauled Anna back to her feet. "Goblins have known of the dragons' ability to speak since the beginning," Shvika said, resuming her pace down the hall. "But who would we tell, since we've been hiding our own existence much longer than dragons have been able to speak?"

Hiro met Anna's eye, but all she could do was shrug her shoulder the tiniest bit.

"I've heard stories," Anna stumbled along the cavern floor, but she tried to get any information she could. "Tales of small, gray-skinned people. We call them elves or—" she hesitated.

"Trolls?" Keeahrspi offered.

"Dwarves?" one of the little yellow-hairs said from behind.

"Phantoms?" the other called.

"Ghosts," Keeahrspi practically growled with an evil grin.

Shvika turned momentarily to her companions and Hiro saw her hide a half-grin. "We go by many names," she said over her shoulder. "Those of us who are careless enough to have our acts noticed, but humans are easily beguiled and likely to believe outrageous stories."

After a few more steps down the sparkling hallway, Shvika came to a shimmering archway decorating the stone wall at a dead end. Without missing a step she walked into the stone under the archway and vanished. Anna gasped, but Keeahrspi pushed her through after his leader. They both vanished.

Hiro slowed his pace, squirming his tail and back end to move away from the archway, but he felt the sting of two blades pointing at his hindquarters. "Keep moving, dragon."

Hiro was tempted to take on the two remaining goblins—surely they wouldn't be much of a match for him—but Anna would be stuck on the other side of the archway without help. So he grit his teeth and moved through it.

After the briefest sensation of weightlessness, Hiro found himself staring at Shvika, Keeahrspi and Anna. An identical archway set into the wall of the large cavern shimmered behind him. He had to take another step forward for his tail to materialize. Then the two yellow-haired goblins stepped through the wall.

Hiro noticed similar archways set into the walls spreading in either direction, some much smaller than the one they had come through, some even larger. Bright yellow banners with more strange markings hung vertically along the left side of each archway.

Mounds of brightly colored spilling stones filled the cavern in front of them. Many were the size of Rakgar and larger and contained tiny doors and windows. Some had hangings with more of the yellow markings over them. Others had cloth squares or boxes outside of them. Hiro expected the scent of stone and rock, but as he pushed further into the cavern he smelled wet earth, as if it had just rained, and the tang of fresh leaf buds on trees.

Small gray people of all shapes and relative sizes stared out at the newcomers. A small gray woman held a little gray baby wrapped in a shimmering red cloth who grabbed at the diminutive mother's plentiful golden necklaces. Her wide eyes got even wider at the sight of the black dragon, but she contained herself and darted behind a bright red door. Braver goblins gaped at him unabashedly, even calling their companions to stare at the marvel.

The ceiling of the magnificent cavern looked identical to the stormy gray clouds in the sky outside, with the same turbulent swirling and shifting overhead. As Hiro stared, it even seemed to be raining, but no water fell. Noticing the black dragon staring up, Keeahrspi grinned at him. "The king enchants the ceiling to reflect the seasons outside. Just because we hide our people doesn't mean we have to miss out on the beauty of nature."

"Is the king—" Anna began, but was cut short when Shvika struck her in the belly with the handle of her sword.

Anna doubled over and croaked as she sucked air back into her lungs. Hiro growled at Shvika, who turned on him. "I allowed her to speak in the tunnels. It will not be tolerated in our home."

Hiro's eyes darted between Shvika and Anna as she coughed and struggled to breathe. Finally he came to a decision. "Violence isn't necessary."

"Humans are violent creatures. We've learned to speak their language," Shvika stated matter-of-factly. She moved ahead of them into the crowd of colorful mounds beyond. "Welcome to Vlist Svorgh."

16

A WYRD

The odd little group marched through the pathways of the goblin homes. Females bedecked in silver and gold and gems jerked children out of their way. Men also covered in precious metals stared with open mouths as they passed. One wrinkled gray-skin actually shrieked when he emerged from his spilling stone mound, only to disappear back inside almost instantly.

Shvika led them past the homes without a single glance. Their progress took them toward the largest mound of stone in the middle of the monstrous cavern. When they approached it, Hiro could see that instead of being a mound, it was a column attached to the top of the cavern. It stood at least seventy dragon lengths tall and more than one hundred dragons would have to stand head-to-tail to encompass it. The outside sparkled with glowing symbols and patterns.

The group of goblins around them stopped at the base of the enormous stone column. Looking up, Hiro could see an opening directly over his head adorned with blue around the edge. Another small, blue-haired goblin peered over the side of the opening briefly, but his eyes widened at the sight of the black dragon. Without a word, he withdrew.

Suddenly the ground shifted from under Hiro's feet. He hated the feeling of the ground leaving him unless by his own will. As he and the others rose into the air, he scrabbled at the air and even the little gray people. He started to open his wings so he could gain control, but Shvika stopped him with one raised hand.

"Don't bother, dragon. You're under our control," she told him.

He tucked his wings again. Trying to keep himself from clawing at the air, he turned to see how Anna fared. Keeahrspi loosened his grip as he floated next to her. She seemed well enough, albeit off-balance, with her arms still tied behind her back. She gave Hiro a slight nod then turned her attention back to the blue opening.

The group floated together, landing just inside the opening as one. More goblins stood around the group with swords drawn. These goblins also wore bright, multi-hued clothes, but their sashes were red with yellow markings instead of the blue ones the group they surrounded wore. The blue-haired goblin had almost as many etchings of blue on his skin as Keeahrspi, along with an excessive amount of small gold rings attached to each ear. One orange-haired goblin with blue framing her face and two red-haired goblins stared at the prisoners with their swords bared. They wore no circlets on their heads.

"I'll take the prisoners from here, Shvika," the blue-haired goblin who had spied them from above spoke.

Shvika didn't even glance at him. "You'll do no such thing, Trosk. Keeahrspi and I will escort them ourselves." She sheathed her small sword and looked Trosk in the eye. "He expects us, I believe."

Trosk seemed to think better of following through with his statement. He dipped his head as he sheathed his sword, and the other goblins did the same. Only Keeahrspi kept his sword out, although by the look in his eye, Hiro couldn't tell if he might use it on the human, the dragon or the other goblins.

The hallway they landed in curved off from either side of the entrance, seeming to encompass the structure. Shvika dismissed Mlika and Morkni to rejoin the others in the tunnel. She and Keeahrspi marched Hiro and Anna further down the hall to the left.

Although painted in the same nauseating, bright colors, the hallways were small, circular and richly adorned with gold and silver in perplexing designs. The same glowing stones that lit the tunnels were attached to these hallways on the sides, top, and hung at evenly spaced intervals in what appeared to be crystal and gold fixings. Hiro slid under these, pressing his battered belly across the glossy, smooth floor.

Instead of following the curving hallway all the way around, Shvika led them to the right past two sets of stairs, one leading up and one leading down. Beyond these, the chamber opened up wide enough for Hiro to fit more comfortably. The glowing stones spiraled up the wall to an even larger golden fixture at least three dragon lengths up. Looking to the left, he saw a stairway wrapped with a dark blue railing with silver spindles leading up to another level. Balconies overhead with the same colored railings opened up into the brightly lit area further above.

Two guards stood at the bottom of the stairs. Keeahrspi heaved Anna, who took the steps two at a time, up the stairs in front of him without sparing Hiro or anyone else a glance. Hiro started to follow them, but stopped when he realized he couldn't navigate the steps with his bulk. He turned to Shvika with a question in his eye.

Shvika jerked her red eyebrows toward the next level up. "Go."

Hiro experimentally opened his wings. Neither wing touched the walls around him, although they came close where he stood, closest to the hallway. Shvika and the other guards covered their faces as he beat his wings and leapt into the air. With just a few wingfalls, he landed on the other side of the blue and silver railings, where Keeahrspi and Anna joined him from the stairs. In front of them was a door large enough for even Rakgar to fit through, decorated with more silver and gold swirls. Two more guards stood on either side.

The trio waited for Shvika to join them. When she finally did, Hiro asked, "Where are you taking us?"

Shvika looked at Keeahrspi. "Sheath your sword," she said, and turned to face the ornate door. "We go before the king."

With a nod from Shvika, the guard to the left opened the door for the odd group. Hiro didn't have time to respond before he was overtaken by the sight beyond. Two more guards with red sashes stood inside the doorway on either side. Drapings with pictures of goblins performing great deeds covered the walls. Another golden fixture hung from the ceiling, this one easily larger than Hiro himself. Motionless gold and silver rivers ran through the floor and curled their way up the walls to the ceiling. But the difference that stood out the most to Hiro was the many gems of multiple hues and sizes and shapes that decorated the wall behind the goblin king.

The king himself sat on a throne completely void of all color or decoration. It threw a shocking contrast to the edifice just as the king's appearance did to the other goblins. Instead of the colorful clothing on most of the other goblins, the king wore only a gray shirt and cloak with brown breeches and muddy brown boots. With his gray skin he might have blended into the rock so flawlessly as to be invisible, if it hadn't been for his bright hair and golden crown.

His long, curly locks, the same blood red as Shvika's, were bound with a royal crown adorned with numerous different colored stones, even climbing the alternating points. They had the same round cut as the gems in Shvika's headpiece and seemed to be placed just as practically, except perhaps the one clear, round stone in the middle of the king's forehead. As the group approached the king, he stared down his bulbous nose at them and shifted on his rigid throne.

"Shvika," he rumbled as they approached, "I knew it would be you." He turned his gaze to the prisoners, but Shvika spoke.

"May I present you to Svorgh, Master and Slave of the Nine Realms, Champion and Challenger of Gem Islands, Elected King and Servant of the Goblins." She and Keeahrspi bent at the waist to bow to the king. "King Svorgh, we found these creatures in the Torthoth entrance."

Hiro decided he should do the talking here. "Your majesty." He bent a knee, carefully dipping himself to the miniscule king. "My name is Hiro Tekla Ido Tusten feira Dakoon." He indicated Anna with a bob of his head. "My companion and I fell into one of your caves when we were attacked by humans. We meant no disrespect or trespass."

The king's eyes shifted under heavy eyebrows to Hiro. "We've had dragons and humans brought to us before. They have all died." He swung his eyes back to Shvika. "What makes these any different?"

Shvika stared back, unafraid. "*Pako sachicha che hobek.*"

As he stood from his bow, Hiro looked to Anna, but she shrugged her shoulders. Neither of them knew what language Shvika spoke, let alone what she'd said.

The king's eyes narrowed at her words and slid back to Hiro. He stared in interminable silence. Finally he spoke in a voice no more than a whisper. "Is this true?" he asked Hiro. "Did you protect this human?"

Hiro lifted with a hope. "Yes."

"Why?" Svorgh demanded.

"She's my travel companion."

"But she's still only a human. She should be your dinner, not your companion!" Svorgh pointed an accusing finger at Anna. "What has she done to deserve such loyalty?"

Hiro declined his head to look at Anna, his tail twitching against the floor. He had no desire to put a voice to his feelings, but he knew he must answer. Turning his eyes from both her and Svorgh, he rolled his shoulder. "She saved my life."

To his surprise, he heard Svorgh chuckle deep in his throat. Svorgh jerked his head at Anna. "And you?" he asked. "Who are you to save a dragon's life?"

Anna's eyes twitched to Shvika and she kept her mouth clamped shut.

Svorgh chuckled again. "Learned the hard lesson, have you?" He motioned to Keeahrspi. "Untie her." He nodded to Shvika. "I give this human permission to speak to the goblins. Let no one harm her, so long as *she* means no harm."

Keeahrspi didn't use his sword to release Anna's bonds. She waited until he untied them by hand. She rubbed her wrists a little before she stood to her full height. Chest out, chin high. "My name is Anna, daughter of King Paudie and Queen Annette, Princess of the Noble Kingdom of Avonoa. I was helping Hiro find the town of Eoaa when we were attacked."

"You search for the Earth Wraith." King Svorgh stood and walked over to Anna. "You carry the means to destroy it." He tapped her side pocket with the back of his hand, exactly where she held the ribbon.

Hiro's eyes narrowed at the king. "How do you know this?"

Svorgh circled Anna, taking in her tattered clothes and wet hair, then stopped directly in front of her. He only came up to her chest, but he glared at her. "As King of the Goblins, you hold no secrets from me."

Anna swallowed. Had her breathing quickened? Hiro wondered what she might be keeping from him, but pushed the thought aside with another roll of his shoulder.

"If you know what we're doing, why have we been brought here?" he asked.

Svorgh rounded on Hiro with a grin. "Dragon ash is highly sought after by many creatures. Some think we mine for gold and gems down here in the earth, but—" he pointed to the gems in his own golden crown, "—these are what we really seek. These gems are different from plain diamonds and rubies. They are made of compressed and hardened dragon ash. We call them dragon stones.

"Each dragon has certain powerful traits while they live. When they die and turn to ash that ash is petrified in the earth and, over thousands of years, turns into these dragon stones. This is where goblins get their power. Not from majik, like the faeries. Not from reading stars, like the centaurs. From the creation of dragon stones."

Hiro cringed. If he and Anna never returned from here, what would become of Tog? Priya? Rakgar? Or any of the dragons?

"Please, Your Majesty," he told the king. "As you must know, Rakgar of the Rock Cloud Ruck sent my friend and me to find this wraith. It has attacked humans and faeries and it's only a matter of time before the dragons are affected by it as well." He couldn't believe Anna's argument sprang from his tongue, but he pushed past it. "It's important that we continue."

"Indeed," Svorgh answered, glancing back at Anna. He nodded slowly to her once before he stepped in front of Hiro. "The Earth Wraith is dangerous and must be dealt with. Besides, turning you into a dragon stone would take far too long. Continue you shall, but not without giving your wyrd never to reveal to another soul the existence of the goblins."

Svorgh resumed his seat on the throne, but when he faced them again a yellow stone on the side of his crown glowed brightly. Hiro tried to ignore it. "I give you my wyrd I will never reveal to another soul the existence of the goblins."

Anna opened her mouth to say the same, but Svorgh held up a hand. "The wyrd of a dragon is indeed a serious oath, but for our custom you must give your wyrd that should you ever reveal our existence," he scowled again at Anna, "you will take each other's lives."

Anna's mouth fell open, but she snapped it shut when she met Hiro's eye. "I give you my wyrd," she said, staring back at Hiro, "on Hiro's life, that I'll never reveal the existence of the goblins to another soul." She looked away from him to the king, who nodded his acceptance.

Hiro grumbled to himself, *It's all very well for her to promise such a thing. She wouldn't stand a chance trying to kill me.* Did Svorgh's lip curl into a smile?

Hiro avoided looking at Anna again. "I give you my wyrd," he told Svorgh, "on Anna's life, that I'll never reveal the existence of the goblins to another soul."

Svorgh's smile spread. "It is well, but I will require an additional oath from you, oh mighty dragon. You must also swear on the life of the dragon known to you as Priya."

Hiro's eyes narrowed. "How do you know Priya?"

"I told you before," Svorgh answered with a grin at Anna, "you hold no secrets from me."

Priya? Hiro's mind raced. "What does she have to do with any of this?"

"She is a dragon you care deeply for, is she not?" Svorgh asked.

"She's not my mate, if that's what you're asking."

Svorgh leaned forward. "No, but I'm sure it's only a matter of time."

Hiro growled and bared his fangs. "Why does everyone keep saying that?" he grumbled, not quite to himself. He crouched low on both front legs, not submissive this time, but in an attack posture. His heart hardened for a second at the thought of such a promise against Priya and he wondered if he did have stronger feelings for her than he realized. But the next moment his heart softened again when he pondered the consequences. "And if I refuse?"

Svorgh frowned at him from under his bushy, red eyebrows. His right hand pointed at Hiro as another red stone on his crown glowed. Hiro felt an invisible force press the rest of his body down to the glossy, golden floor. He couldn't move. He felt as if he lay chained in the courtyard of Kingstor Noble again. "If you refuse," Svorgh's deep voice sliced the air, "you will both die now. You will not return to your friend, Toggil, on the surface and the wraith will lay waste to the land." Svorgh put his hand back on his thigh and the red stone stopped glowing. Hiro's unseen bonds loosed and he sprang to his feet. "Or do you plan to break your wyrd, Hiro Tekla?"

Hiro didn't know why he chose this moment to be so protective of Priya. She didn't need to know about anything happening in this brightly lit cavern. No one need ever know any of this happened.

Hiro dipped his head again, but didn't bend his knee. "I give you my wyrd, King Svorgh, on the life of Priya as well as Anna, that I will never reveal the existence of the goblins to another soul."

"Was that so hard?" Keeahrspi whispered.

The yellow stone in Svorgh's crown ceased its glow. "Good." The king fell silent. He stroked the blood-red point of the beard dripping from his chin, eyeing the dragon. With his eyes locked on Hiro's, his voice softened to a whisper, "*Nazhelsa nasay prema ha has.*" Shvika shared a brief glance with Keeahrspi before the king spoke again. "Escort them back to the surface at the base of the Trangoth Mountain to rejoin their companion."

"Yes, sir," the two goblins answered and bowed.

As they turned to leave the great hall, Svorgh called out, "Hiro!" His voice rumbled like an earthquake. Hiro snaked his head back and looked at the king. "Be careful who you trust."

Hiro wondered if he meant Anna, but the king's large black eyes never wavered from Hiro's. Hiro dipped his head in response and followed Shvika from the chamber.

———

Shvika and Keeahrspi brought them to the surface through a different archway. Fewer tunnels ran from this one. Keeahrspi kept Anna walking in front of him. As they walked back, Hiro's questions overflowed.

"Why did he let us go?" he asked Shvika as only the sound of their feet against the floor could be heard.

"Would you rather go back?" she asked without slowing her pace.

"No, but…"

"My father does things for his own reasons," she said. "As king, he has access to amazing power and knowledge. They often change the elected one."

"Your father?" Anna asked. When Shvika nodded, she said, "How long has he been king?"

"He was elected twelve years ago. He only has one year left on the throne."

"Will you be queen next?"

Both Shvika and Keeahrspi laughed. "Unlike the humans, goblin royalty doesn't follow bloodlines," she answered. "I would only ever become queen through my merits and my own election." She dropped her voice. "At least, if I wanted it."

The goblins stopped suddenly when a distant light shone ahead of them. It took Anna a few steps to realize the others weren't following. Hiro loped next to Shvika and behind the other two, so he stopped beside them.

"The opening is ahead." Shvika pointed with her sword. "You'll come out behind a large boulder." She placed her finger to her head and closed her eyes. A pale green stone glowed ever so slightly as she swung her head from side to side. The glowing stopped and she opened her eyes. "Your gray friend is further north, but not far." The goblins turned on their heels.

"That's it?" Hiro asked.

Shvika slowed and stopped. She turned back only part way to speak to him. "Unfortunately, I feel that we'll see each other again." Both her large eyes met his. "Until then, good luck."

"Wait," Hiro called, before they could disappear. When Shvika turned again to hear him, he asked. "What did he say?" Shvika peered at him with ice-cold, gray eyes. "What did the king say before he told you to bring us here? What language was it he spoke?"

She continued to stare at him until he felt she would never answer, then she sighed. "Goblin tongue is older than Faerie tongue," she whispered. "And he said, 'It seems our time is upon us.'" With that, the two goblins seemed to run away as fast as they could.

17

WEST

When Hiro and Anna emerged from the boulder, rain fell in a misty spray. Hiro could only see a heavy fog around them interspersed with trees. He looked north, but couldn't see Tog. "Come on," he whispered to Anna. "Stay close."

He tip-taloned between the trees, moving along the mountain line. Glancing back, he saw Anna far behind him, struggling to find footing to follow. Her arms wrapped tight around her shoulders and her hair, which had dried partially in the tunnels, once again took on the sleek, wet-cat look he'd grown accustomed to. She shivered as she set her foot down, yanked it back up, and winced again as she slid it carefully into another spot.

Hiro peered into the trees around them, but stayed still while she caught up to him. When she finally stepped

142

gingerly next to his tail, he laid his belly flat on the muddy ground. "Get on," he whispered.

"What?" she asked through chattering teeth.

"Get on my back." He rolled his shoulder. "I can't wait for you to pick your way through the forest. Climb on before I change my mind."

Anna must have realized how serious he was, because she didn't question him further. Straddling his tail first, she clambered up his spine and came to rest between his wings. Hiro lifted his wings slightly while she settled, then wrapped them back against his sides, covering her legs to hold her tight against him.

"Stay low and be quiet," he said, continuing his way back toward the mountain. He felt her lay down against his scales and marveled at how he barely felt her weight. As he loped along silently, he worried that another human might see them. He had no way of explaining the odd sight any more than Anna might. It would be difficult enough to explain to Tog.

As they rounded another large boulder on their right, Hiro heard Anna whisper. "There, to the right." He twisted around enough to see in his peripheral vision where she pointed. Following her finger, he saw something that looked like another large boulder, but it had a long tail and spikes running down the center. Tog.

Hiro snuck up behind his friend, but called to him before they got too close. Tog snapped his head around at the sound. The one eye looking at them widened. He looked around cautiously and snaked his way toward them.

"What do you think you're doing?" he growled low at Hiro. "Where have you been?"

"We've been looking for you, you troll," Hiro growled back. "Remind me to leave you behind next time."

"Get that thing off your back," Tog stared hard into Hiro's face. "You look like a common mule."

He felt Anna shift on his back as if to move, so he lifted his wings to release her. "She moves too slow on foot," he told Tog. "I had to do something."

"I'll be fine," Anna said once she slid down his tail and stood next to the dragons. "We should get into the air, anyway."

Hiro examined Tog's front leg and belly where he'd been hit with the arrows from the human attack. "Your wounds?"

"Burned out. Yours?"

"Anna pulled them out." Which was only partially a lie. Anna had pulled out one and Shvika pulled out the others.

"Right. Let's hit the sky." Hiro opened his claw and Anna curled into her customary ball, but something was missing. "Where's your hide? And your food?" he asked her.

She suddenly seemed very interested in tucking her skirt under her knees. "I lost it. All of it," she said. She finally looked into his eyes. "In the cave."

Hiro remembered she had thrown everything aside before they were taken prisoner by the goblins. She didn't have anything with her in the vast goblin city of Vlist Svorgh.

Tog moaned softly. "What cave?"

After a moment, Hiro met his friend's gaze. "We took shelter in a small cave at the base of the cliff. We hid there until the humans left."

"Well, what do we do now?" Tog bared his fangs at Hiro. "This human continues to slow us down. Now we have to go back and search for her blanket?"

"No," Anna answered before Hiro could say anything. "We're not far from Eoaa now. I'll get new supplies there, if I can. If not, I'll go without."

Tog didn't answer. He growled and searched the branches above for an escape. Hiro knew his friend didn't want to admit that Anna wasn't the human that was slowing them down.

Luckily the sparse forest around them didn't have thick coverage. Tog bobbed his head at an opening. As the group limped toward it, Hiro whispered to Anna, but loud enough for Tog to hear, too. "This time, I'm flying west on purpose."

18

REQUESTS

"It seems very extreme," Torgon said, tapping the hilt of his sword and leaning against the door frame between the two offices. "Until a few months ago, I would have sworn no faerie would ever allow any harm to come to a dragon. They protected them for so long, as if they were sacred animals. Why have the faeries suddenly decided all dragons must be killed?"

"That's what worries me most." Philip paced in his large office. "A gradual change I could understand, but this is so abrupt. I just wanted you to know I'm going to question them about it."

Torgon stood up straight. "Do you want me to be present?"

"No," Philip shook his head. He would have been grateful for Torgon's support, but didn't want this meeting to start off hostile. "I just thought you should know ahead of time in case the situation takes a turn for the worse."

Torgon nodded. "I have some promotions to attend. I'll be at the training ground if you need me." Without all the pomp of bowing and saluting, Torgon turned back into his office and closed the door. Philip enjoyed the familiarity they shared with no one else around. He knew Torgon saw him as a person. An equal.

A few minutes later, a knock came at the door which led to the audience chamber. Once invited, Murthur entered and closed the door behind him. "The faeries await you, Sire," he said, bowing slightly.

"Thank you." Philip set down the list of names of men currently preparing to leave on the faerie expedition then leaned back in his chair to stare at the ceiling.

"Sire?" Murthur said after an interval.

"Yes?"

"Should I ask them to come back another time?"

"I sent for them," Philip said, still contemplating the ceiling. "Why would I now send them away?"

Murthur crossed his hands behind his back and waited. After another interlude, he asked, "Will you go out to them, Sire?"

After another long moment, Philip sighed. The insolent faeries had waited long enough. Philip stood. "My cloak." He allowed Murthur to drape the rich, velvet cloak over his shoulders and brush him off. Eventually, Philip led the way into the audience chamber.

The two faeries stood in the middle of the room. Kradik's back was to Philip and by the tilt of their heads, Philip knew he had interrupted a conversation. Perhaps

Kradik was trying to convince Qialla to leave, seeing as they were made to wait so long.

Good, Philip thought, *they know I am not at their leisure.*

"Gentlemen," Philip addressed them as he would nobility, but he didn't take his throne as he did with a typical audience. Instead he approached them directly. "I have some questions for you before we can proceed."

Kradik turned to face Philip, but with the ever-present cloak and face trappings, he couldn't look him in the eye. "What kind of questions?" the faerie snapped.

Philip tried to stare into the dark recesses of the cloak, but still found it unnerving that Kradik could confront him with so much frankness. So he returned in kind. "I have concerns about your motives, to be quite honest."

Kradik took a sharp breath, but before he could blurt out whatever retort he formed, Qialla stopped him with a raised hand. "What's wrong with our motives, King Philip?"

Philip grudgingly shifted his gaze to the Faerie Councilman. "When Kradik and Ortym arrived here a few months ago, they claimed it was to help the Noble Kingdom and keep balance in Avonoa. However, I can't help but feel bothered by the insistence on killing every dragon. Killing one stray dragon is dangerous enough, but you want me to help you wipe out the entire species." Philip stood to his full height, bringing his eyes to the tops of the faeries' heads. "I'm sorry, but I'm going to need more confirmation that you represent the whole of the faerie kingdoms."

"You received a letter from the Faerie Council, did you not?" Qialla said.

"Letters are easily written."

"The entire Faerie Council signed it."

"Signatures can be forged."

"Forged?!" Kradik burst out.

Qialla held up his hand again. "Not faerie signatures."

The tapestry across the room caught Philip's eye. "Gentlemen," he motioned toward it, "the faeries once came to aid humans in another great time of need. My ancestors fought savage wars against other humans." He stared at the bloody bodies in the background of the tapestry. What might it have been like to live in such a horrific time as that? "The faeries brought us these gifts." He indicated the focal point of the artwork: the faeries, with delicate pink skin, pointed ears and humble, down-cast eyes, giving a shining sword to five human men dressed in the colors from the five kingdoms of Avonoa. "They brought us peace. A peace we have enjoyed for over two thousand years."

He turned back to the dark-hooded faeries. "But even then, the human kings and queens had to be brought together. They had to talk to each other face-to-face." Philip crossed his hands behind his back. "I want to trust you, gentlemen. My men are gathering supplies. They'll be ready to depart within a week, but I need assurances that this project isn't just the fancy of a rogue councilmember."

Kradik mumbled under his breath. Philip desperately prayed he wasn't about to find himself on the receiving end of a curse. Perhaps he should have had

Travaith, his own majishun, accompany him. Finally, Qialla nodded.

"Very well, Your Majesty." He turned toward the giant double doors leading out of the audience chamber. "Come with me."

"Where are we going?" Philip asked as he hurried to match Qialla's swift gait.

"I hope your cloak will be warm enough for you."

The cloak had only been another tactic to slow him down at the time, but now he was grateful he'd put it on at all. "Are we going outside?"

"Yes."

"Why?"

"I assume you wish to speak to the Faerie Council yourself."

"Myself?" Philip wanted to kick himself for asking.

"Of course," Qialla barked from a pace ahead of him. "How else would you confirm our credentials?"

In truth, Philip had hoped to write a letter to the Faerie Council asking for specifics and hopefully opening a dialogue to attempt to sway the faeries from their current course of action. He hoped it would delay either the men leaving on their journey or any more dragon poison being made. If a vengeance-crazed dragon truly was headed for his kingdom, he didn't want to weaken his forces any more than absolutely necessary.

When Philip didn't offer an immediate reply, Qialla continued. "I'll take you to the platform from which I contact the council for reports on our progress. You can speak to them yourself."

What, now? Philip was too awed by the thought to respond. He knew faerie majik to be powerful, but to speak directly with someone thousands of wingfalls away as the dragon flies must be impossible. Could it possibly be a trick?

Qialla's quick pace told otherwise. Besides, Philip had only just shared his concerns with them. They had not been out of his presence since. They couldn't have put together an illusion so quickly without his being aware. Could they?

The faeries led Philip down the southeast tower stair. He attempted to remain regal while hurrying to stay in step. He ignored his own personal edict and avoided looking into the eyes of the bewildered guards they whisked passed.

They practically flew down the tower, down a few more hallways, then out an exterior door just under the opening to the training grounds. After stopping at the base of the castle on the rocky shoreline leading to Teardrop Sea, Philip followed the faeries into the drizzling rain. Ahead of them, an ordinary wooden platform sat in the middle of the rocks. A shallow silver dish about six hand lengths across gently splashed the rain back into the air. With a wave of his gloved hand, Qialla motioned Philip toward it.

Philip threw his cowl over his head and approached the platform. It was only large enough to accommodate two people. When he put out his foot to step onto it, Qialla immediately did the same. Once their feet touched the boards, the platform rose smoothly into the air. Philip tried not to cry out or react in any way. He knew that displaying any shock or surprise at such majik would lessen his character even further in the faeries' eyes.

"These platforms are made by majikal means," Qialla said, peering at the view. As they stood together Philip noted Qialla's dry cloak. Not that it beaded and rolled off; the rain falling didn't touch the material at all. "Normally we use majikally charmed animals to relay messages. I personally prefer to rely on snakes. But this vessel allows council members immediate communication. Altitude is important in communication majik, but if we fly, we might drift. We plan to build more of these platforms for humans to use against the dragons; thus removing one of the dragons' major advantages."

Luckily, Philip had no qualms with heights. The platform soared into the air past the training grounds to shouts of amazement. It glid past the castle, level with the roof of the southeast tower. The guards below them pointed and cried out, but Philip tried to ignore them. Realizing he had received no reports on the faeries' use of such a contraption, he suspected they must have taken pains to keep the information hidden. More reason not to trust them. He stored these thoughts away to discuss with Torgon later.

Once the platform slowed to hover over the trees, Qialla lifted the silver dish. The dish displayed ornate scrollwork around the edges. Philip recognized some of it as Faerie tongue. The rest looked like decoration in the form of waves on water, but he couldn't be sure.

"It will take most of my energy and concentration to sustain the spell," Qialla said. "I'll only be capable of a short communication." Qialla whispered a few words into the dish, which held a finger's depth of water in the bottom.

As Philip watched, the water in the bottom of the dish lifted free from it. The ball of water poised in the air in front of the two men. Qialla continued to whisper the words of the spell. Philip could hear the tell-tale cadence of majik. He had to resist the temptation of tapping his foot in time with any majishun's incantation.

Finally, Qialla's voice faded as an image of another faerie appeared in the floating water. This faerie didn't wear the cloak and face covering that Qialla and Kradik wore. The faerie they were looking at must be somewhere among other faeries.

Qialla didn't wait for a question. He stared blankly into the orb of floating water. "King Philip wishes to speak to the Faerie Council. Now." He tilted his face down to the platform they stood on and continued his chant in a low tone.

The other faerie disappeared from the orb. Philip focused on the view of a glittering room. He could see the wood-grain lines of a tree behind shimmering gossamer draping. A soft light spread over the scene from somewhere above. Two gracefully carved couches adorned with plush pillows were arranged in front of the hangings against the far wall. A fragile tea service perched on a table between them.

Just as Philip began to inspect the lush rug on the floor, the faerie reappeared. He bowed silently and motioned to Philip with a wave of his hand. Then the faerie disappeared again as five other faeries came into view.

The five figures filled the scene in the orb. They all threw their hoods over their heads, but didn't bother to add the face mask, so Philip could see their chins and mouths as they spoke. The hems of their hoods and cloaks had intricate scrollwork around them, similar to the cloak Qialla wore but in different colors. The faerie in a cloak with a bright green design spoke first. Philip could see straight teeth set in a square jaw surrounded by pitch-black hair. He placed his hand on his chest and Philip could also see the muscles, bones and tendons of his ungloved hand. "I am Paliodor of the Faerie Council," he nodded to Philip.

"I am Marunda of the Faerie Council," the next faerie said.

"I am Transil of the Faerie Council."

"I am Brussi of the Faerie Council."

"I am Horatio of the Faerie Council," the last faerie, with silver hair suspended next to a long slim neck, introduced himself.

Philip nodded in kind. He had seen all their names signed at the bottom of many letters recently. "I am King Philip of the Noble Kingdom of Avonoa. I'm pleased to speak to our allies of the faeries, but it seems there is one member missing."

Two of the faeries nodded, but Paliodor spoke. "Yes, Skorkot is away on another assignment. What is the purpose of this communication, King Philip?" he asked. "We did not plan on hearing from you directly."

"I'm feeling uneasy about the course set before us," Philip told them. "I need direct assurance that Qialla has permission to speak on your behalf."

"He has our full trust," Marunda said.

"When one of the Faerie Council speaks," Brussi said, "we all speak."

"What are your concerns, King Philip?" Paliodor asked.

"I fear that attacking the dragons is too dangerous for humans, even with faerie majik to assist us." His words had a surprising effect.

Two of the faeries actually began to turn away. One bared his teeth past invisible lips; Philip thought that one was Transil. They all stirred.

"The dragons are a plague on the land," Marunda stated.

"They should all be destroyed," Horatio whispered and Brussi nodded vehemently next to him.

Paliodor raised his hand. "Peace," he told the council, then he addressed Philip. "The dragons have…killed our citizens as well as humans."

"But why have the faeries had this sudden change of heart?" Philip asked. "Until Kradik and Ortym showed up here a few months ago, any human would have guessed that a faerie would rather die than harm a dragon."

"This change has been coming in our community for some time now." As Paliodor said this, Marunda snapped her head to look in his direction. "We have seen the destruction these creatures create. It can't be allowed for a peaceful world any longer." Marunda turned back to look at Philip.

"But they're just animals," Philip said. "A dog can be dangerous in the wild, too. We've shared this world with the dragons and many other species for all time. Why should we turn on them now?"

Paliodor stepped forward. "Are you saying you would allow a dragon power over your people?"

"Of course not."

"Dragons," Paliodor said through grit teeth, "are more than just dangerous. They are a mindless blight that needs to be wiped off the face of this land."

As Philip mentally gaped at the Faerie Council, the bubble he stared into began to droop.

"This communication has gone on too long and taken Qialla's strength," Paliodor pointed out. Philip glanced at Qialla, who stooped at his side. "Do you have any further questions, Your Majesty?"

Philip shook his head.

"Know this in parting," Paliodor lifted his chin. "Qialla is our voice in all matters. If you disagree with him, you disagree with all of us and in turn the entire faerie race. No one wants a conflict between faeries and humans."

Philip clenched his fists under his cloak. "I understand."

All five faeries nodded their heads as Paliodor said, "Farewell, King Philip of the Noble Kingdom of Avonoa. Good fortune be on you."

19

ATTACK IN EOAA

"There!" Anna yelled from Hiro's fist. Rain beat so hard on the dragons' scales that all of them were forced to yell to be heard at all. He looked in the direction she pointed as she said, "I can see the houses."

Hiro turned to Tog, who nodded, then back to Anna. "Let's find some cover."

The two dragons dipped their right wings slightly. Hiro pulled Anna up against his chest to hide her from view as much as possible. As they dropped lower, Tog snorted. Hiro turned to see Tog push his nose toward a large clump of trees on the southernmost part of the little village. Hiro nodded and the pair dropped quickly into the trees.

The trees provided ample cover, but they were uncomfortably close to the human homes. Only a fragile wooden framework stood between the two dragons and the modest little dwellings. The rain assailed everything around them, but failed to cover the sweet smell of animal flesh within the frame. In the dwellings beyond, two small shutters at a window hung open with a flickering glimmer inside.

The noise of the pounding rain covered the two dragons' bumbling in the bracken. Hiro lost his footing upon landing and dumped Anna into prickly bush. Although she jumped upright again with her mouth wide, she contained any urge to scream. Once she gained her bare feet, she kicked Hiro with one of them. The group pressed through the brush to peer out into the little village of Eoaa.

"Now what?" Anna whispered.

Hiro crouched low to the ground with his feet tucked under him. He twisted his head to look at Tog. "Perhaps you should take a look around," he said to his friend. "Anna and I will watch from here."

Ordinarily Hiro wouldn't presume to give orders to Tog, but they both knew that Tog's eyes were better in the dark and in the rain. Tog could pass anything he saw to Hiro and it would be as if Hiro had seen it himself. Tog nodded and disentangled himself from the bushes. He set out around the village, crawling low to the ground and stopping occasionally to peer around. Hiro lost sight of him as he rounded another framework.

"What do we do?" Anna asked.

"We wait."

"Wait for what?"

"To see if the wraith shows up."

Anna folded her arms across her body. "Well, you're just a master strategist, aren't you?" She jerked her chin to the little home. "Who's in there?"

Hiro stretched his neck up to look into the open shutters of the house. Over the edge of the opening, he could see a small boy bundled under a thick layer of cloth. The boy reminded Hiro of Harry, the little boy who unwittingly stumbled upon Hiro (or Dak, as he had been called then) outside of Jarek's village some months ago. He knew it couldn't be the same child, but all these smaller humans looked alike to a dragon. Big heads, little bodies, big eyes. He thought of the scrunched-up face little Harry made when he attempted to fly like a dragon when this young boy scrunched up his face as well.

Hiro felt something touch his front leg. "Lift me up so I can see." He realized Anna had tried to hit him and stifled a laugh.

Without a word, he scooped up Anna with his front claw and lifted her to the height of his head. As he did, a curtain within the human dwelling was pushed aside and a larger human female holding a little bowl appeared. Anna braced herself by grabbing one of the horns that curved off the back of Hiro's head. Hiro pulled himself and Anna back slightly, making sure they were in shadow, but it wasn't needed. The woman didn't even glance out the window.

The human woman set the bowl on the floor next to where the boy cuddled under the blankets. She pulled a rag out of the bowl and squeezed it. Sitting next to the boy, she pressed the rag to his forehead. Anna gasped.

"He must be sick," she whispered.

"What's she doing?"

"Probably trying to heal him," she answered. She pushed away from Hiro's head to look at him. "Don't dragons get sick?"

Hiro shook his head. "Never." Anna snorted and Hiro fought another grin.

The two watched in silence as the woman administered to the young boy. Again and again she dabbed at his forehead with the cloth. They watched the village streets beyond the home, but only once did they see another human run through the rain before disappearing again.

After what seemed like most of the night—or day, or whatever—Tog returned from the other direction. Anna huddled between Hiro's front legs to avoid the rain as he approached. He gave Hiro a scathing look, but Hiro just shook his head.

"How does it look out there?" Hiro asked.

"Quiet," Tog hunched his shoulders, "very quiet. It seems most of the homes are empty."

"Empty?"

"Yes," Tog scanned the houses again. "It looks as if most of the humans have gone."

"Are they dead?" Hiro asked.

Tog shook his head. "I didn't see any bodies."

"Graves?" Anna asked.

Hiro tipped his head upside down to stare at her. She poked her head out from between his legs. "Humans don't turn into ash when they die. We dig holes in the ground and put the bodies of our dead in them, then cover them with the dirt."

Tog twisted his face at that. "I didn't see any fresh mounds, either." He shook his head. "It seems like the humans are just—gone."

"It makes sense," Anna said, slipping out from under Hiro's belly. "If King Torodov saw the path of death leading in a certain direction, he would tell his people to get out of the way."

"But there are still humans here," Tog gestured to the houses.

"They must not be able to travel." She pointed to the house in front of them. "Like the mother with a sick child. They can't leave. She probably can't move him or she would risk him becoming sicker."

"Then they'll be the wraith's next meal," Tog said, curling up on the ground.

"But…" Anna started to ask Tog, then turned to Hiro, "surely you're not just going to sit there and let these people die?"

"What am I supposed to do?" Hiro asked her.

"Help them!" Anna put her hand on Hiro's leg. "Shampy said the wraith fears dragon fire. You could easily frighten it away." She reached into her pocket and pulled out the ribbon. "We have the means; we could kill it now."

Tog didn't even raise his head from his claws. "With whose help?" he muttered. "Yours?"

"Yes, mine," Anna hissed over her shoulder at him. When she turned her sad eyes on Hiro, he avoided them by staring into the window of the mother and sick child.

He only debated with himself a moment, then softened his heart against all the humans, even the one standing next to him. "And what would they say to their king when the wraith was destroyed?" He looked back down at Anna. "How would they explain two dragons and the Princess Noble saving their lives?"

Anna's hand dropped along with her jaw. "You'll let them die?"

Hiro couldn't answer. He felt the same guilt he'd felt when he left little Harry behind when he chose instead to hunt for Priya. But Tog answered for him. "We're here to find out more about this creature. Nothing more." He lifted his head to look straight into Anna's face. "We'll do nothing without orders from Rakgar."

"I shudder to think what might happen if you get hungry before you get back to the Rock Clouds." She spun on her heel to crawl back between Hiro's claws and muttered, "Will you starve to death without orders to eat?"

—

The three of them nestled in the trees next to the village of Eoaa. The pounding rain turned into a light drizzle. Hiro curled on his side, but held his front leg and part of his wing over Anna. He watched the pathway leading through the village for any sign of life.

"Perhaps Shampy was wrong," Tog mumbled.

"Maybe we're too late," Anna offered. "Maybe no one left, they—" Before she could finish a scream sounded in the distance.

The two dragons' heads hurdled into the air. Anna sprang to her feet. "Or perhaps Shampy was right," Hiro whispered.

Another weaker scream sounded in the distance then was strangled until it ceased altogether. The woman in the house had heard it, too. Hiro watched as she ran to the candles in the room and doused them. He could just make out her figure as she flung herself on the bed over her child.

Tog took a measured step to the side. He watched down the street while Anna pressed herself against Hiro's side.

"What do you see?" Hiro whispered to Tog.

He waited for a response. He could feel Anna shaking next to him; she hadn't shaken this badly in all the time they'd been together. He felt the urge to curl himself around her, but instead stayed still enough to hear everything happening. The animals before them squealed madly, running around their pen and even digging at its edges to get out. He could faintly make out the sounds of the woman whispering a quiet song to the little boy with the rag on his head.

"Hiro," Anna breathed next to him, "you have to do something! You have to stop this!"

Horses down the path exploded in resounding cries. Then silence. The woman whimpered softly and the child moaned.

Finally Tog crept backward. He stretched his neck, without any unnecessary movement, and stopped in front of Hiro. He breathed a short, hot breath.

Hiro looked down the dark street with clarity he could only have while seeing through Tog's eyes. He saw the rain dripping from the eaves of buildings. It seemed like an empty pathway until a dark figure drifted from a building. The figure seemed to struggle, leading with its head first, as if it strained against a strong wind that might whip it away. In the shadows it couldn't be described as male or female. It had no face, only a dark mass for a body, the shape of a head on top and the possibility of arms or hands at its sides. Its bottom half hung like a black waterfall cascading over the ground, never touching it except for one long, thin, spectral, trail of shadow stretching behind.

Hiro blinked to find himself staring into Tog's eyes, but Tog moved away slowly to look back out into the street.

"Please, Hiro," Anna's voice broke, "please…"

"I can't," he snapped at her. He turned to look her straight in the eye. "They're just humans."

She threw her eyes to the ground and Hiro turned back to watch the woman and the little boy. As his eyes adjusted to the darkness in her room, he could barely make out the curtain on the wall. A dark shape drifted in front of it. Without having pushed it aside, the wraith entered the room noiselessly.

Hiro expected the woman to offer up the little boy to the creature for her own safety. He even expected to watch as she left the boy behind and jumped out the window to run away. What he didn't expect was exactly what she did. Hiro saw the form of the woman jump from the bed, fling her arms wide and place herself between the wraith and the child.

Why would she do that? Hiro thought. *That's a very dragonish thing to do.*

Anna must have seen the wraith in the room, too. "No," she whispered and took a step toward the house. She drew in a deep breath, but Hiro caught her in midair before she could throw herself forward. Holding one claw over her face and wrapping the other around her body, he pulled her into his chest. She flailed wildly in his claw, but Hiro barely noticed.

He watched as the wraith lifted the woman from the ground with its hands on either side of her head without actually touching her. The woman screamed and a visible stream of air, like steam issuing from a fresh kill in winter, drifted from woman to monster. The wraith closed its fists in the air and the woman crumpled on the ground.

Hiro ground his teeth as the wraith approached the child. Weak as he was, he offered no resistance. He lolled in the air as the beast sucked the life from him. His body fell to the floor alongside his mother's. The wraith then drifted through the window into the pen where the beasts still thrashed around, desperate for freedom. One at a time, the monster lifted each of the six, sucked the life from them, and left them lifeless in the mud.

The dragons watched silently from the trees. Hiro held Anna tightly against his chest. Her screams of protest transformed into sobs as the scene unfolded before them. Instead of hitting Hiro with her tiny fists, she pressed her hands against her face.

In the silence, Anna's sobs echoed through the night. When the monster's head searched in the direction of the trees, Hiro squeezed Anna tighter. He dropped his head next to hers. "Quiet," he breathed gently.

The wraith struggled against the invisible force binding him, pushing toward the trees.

"It knows you're here," Hiro whispered.

Anna's head snapped up. She silenced her choking cry.

The wraith pushed itself to the right, then the left. It even drifted backward at one point, but continued to move closer and closer to the trees.

Hiro felt Anna trying to free herself from his grasp, but he clutched her even tighter. The wraith was less than a dragon's length away from them. Hiro covered half that distance by stretching his neck out in front of him. He growled low in case there were any other humans around, but he allowed some of his fire to rise in his throat. It glittered between his pointed teeth, tickling his lips. Faster than he would have thought possible, the wraith retraced its path back through the humans' home and into the night.

20

INTELLIGENT COMPARISONS

Anna sat in the mud, muffling her sobs for several minutes. Finally able to control herself, she got to her feet. "I'm going to search the village," she muttered.

"It might still be out there," Hiro answered, although he was fairly certain it had gone.

"Then give me a light to search by," she said without meeting his eye.

Hiro broke off a tree branch. Pointing it toward the mud at his feet so as not to light the whole forest, he bathed it in fire long enough to reach the dry center.

As quietly as possible, Anna slipped out of the trees to the road beyond, holding the burning branch in her fist. When Tog followed without protest, Hiro knew he thought the worst, too. But curiosity overtook Hiro. He stepped lightly over the wooden framework in front of them, past the carcasses, and put his head through the window of the human home.

The woman and her son lay still on the dirty floor with glassy eyes staring back at him. Hiro put his nose next to the woman's face and nudged her icy cheek. He sniffed over the floor around them, then the bed where the boy had lain and the candle.

When he pulled his head back out of the window and into the rain, Tog stared at him.

"What is it?" Tog asked.

"The candle," Hiro said, "it was lit with dragon fire. If she'd left it to burn, it might have saved their lives."

"Or it might not have," Tog stated. "It was a small flame."

Hiro couldn't answer.

"Can you pick up the wraith's scent?" Tog whispered.

Hiro shook his head. "It has no scent."

"Hiro!" Anna called from around the corner of the house.

"Shhh!" Tog breathed.

Hiro and Tog crept around the home and into the street. Tog kept his body low to the ground and both eyes scanning the buildings around them.

"There's no one else," Anna said. "I found an old man and woman. Another woman and three children. All dead."

"I'm sorry, Anna," Hiro offered, but only received a disdainful look from Tog.

"It's alright," she shook her head. "I think I understand your limitations. I'm going to find some warmer clothes and maybe some food for myself." He nodded as she turned and ran into one of the nearby buildings.

"It's time we take her home," Tog said when she left.

Hiro sighed. "I agree."

"It will only be more dangerous for all of us if she continues with us."

"I know."

Tog laid his head down on his front claws. Hiro did the same, but he was sure the position was the only thing the same about their attitudes. Hiro knew Anna must go back, but he felt as if he would be abandoning her. No, not her. He felt the sting of the memory of watching the little boy die. He had felt bad enough when he had to leave Harry behind to be punished, but forcing Anna to allow this boy's death prickled at his heart. He couldn't explain why these little humans had such a flustering effect on him. Perhaps he could sense an innocence in them. Perhaps they shouldn't be forced to learn to become monsters like their parents. Except this woman hadn't been a monster.

Tog's eyes eventually closed, but Hiro could only watch him sleep. As much as he wanted to help Anna and the little humans, his claws were bound by his wyrd. He had given his wyrd to Rakgar never to speak to or interact with humans. Every dragon gave this oath when they passed the Krusible. He knew the dangers humans brought. He experienced their brutality, had he not? How could he ever help them?

And yet Anna was willing to work with him. Could there possibly be any other humans who wouldn't victimize a dragon immediately upon sight? He had only experienced their harshest cruelty. Yet he had watched the human woman place herself in harm's way trying to protect her child. Her actions went against everything Hiro had ever been taught about humans and everything he'd taught the hatchlings. Was there more to humans than any dragon knew? His mind replayed the memory of the human abusers filing past him in the castle courtyard, but Jarek walked past with his hands stuffed deep in his pockets.

———

Eventually Hiro must have drifted off to sleep. He woke to a thunderclap overhead and Anna racing through the torrential rain toward him.

"I'm sorry!" she yelled over the sloshing. "I found an empty bed and must have fallen asleep."

Hiro looked into the sky, but couldn't guess at the time of day or night. "We should leave," he said.

"I've got everything I need." Anna held up a bag slung over one shoulder and Hiro noticed the thick cloak wrapped around her. She even had strong leather bindings on her feet and legs. "I'll be much more comfortable now."

"Well, thank Shurta for that," Tog moaned, stretching his neck. "We wouldn't want the fragile little human to get cold."

The dragons lifted easily into the sky from the middle of the village road. No humans saw them come or go. Once they were well into the air, they shifted their course toward Kingstor Noble.

"Where are we going?" Anna asked, looking around from Hiro's claw.

Hiro glanced at Tog before answering. "We're taking you home."

He could feel her breathing intensify, but her voice was steady when she asked, "Why?"

"It's too dangerous for the three of us to continue keeping company," Hiro said. "For you and for us."

"But I have no hope of tracking this creature on my own." She stared up at him, but Hiro avoided her eyes.

"The wraith has no scent," he explained. "We can't track it ourselves."

"But we have to kill it together." Her voice began to rise. "You have the fire and I have the ribbon."

Hiro couldn't argue that point with her, but he knew Tog had no intention of pursuing the wraith. He couldn't answer her, so Tog did it for him.

"We won't act until we report back to Rakgar," Tog said.

"Oh, I see," she said, releasing her hold on Hiro's front leg to cross her arms firmly. "You're going to use the excuse of having to report to your king in order to hide your cowardice."

"Careful, woman," Tog growled with teeth bared. Hiro resisted the urge to pull Anna closer. "I might get hungry."

No one spoke for the rest of the day. Anna sat in Hiro's claw silently, but he could almost hear her teeth grinding. When they came to Yiksee, they skirted the village far to the west and flew further south along the Torthoth Mountains than where they had approached.

Upon drawing near the mountains, Anna finally called to Hiro. "We need to land," she said. When he wrinkled his forehead at her request, she said, "Trust me. I'll explain on the ground."

Tog rolled an eye at him, but followed as he descended. They landed in the Black Forest next to a large pond with trees and boulders around its shore.

"Alright," Hiro put Anna on her feet, "what are we doing?"

His attitude didn't help. She wrapped her cloak around her. "You would think you'd have learned your lesson the first time you were shot."

"You mean the lesson that I should have dropped you and flown away?" He nodded. "Yes, I learned that lesson."

"My brother has patrols out." She locked her icy gaze on him. "They're sure to be spread out along the mountains watching for you. The rain is letting up and you'll be seen if we fly over in the daytime."

The two dragons looked into the sky. The rain had been lifting and Hiro could feel the change in the air. Although the rains of fall rarely stopped completely, he knew they would ease for a while. He looked around at their location, avoiding Anna's eyes, as Tog did the same.

Finally Tog's and Hiro's eyes met. Tog muttered a curse and curled himself on the ground with his back to Anna. Hiro sighed, "Alright." He reluctantly met her smug grin. "We'll leave at dark."

Anna just grinned and sat on the cold ground leaning against a boulder. Tog lifted his head when Hiro stepped closer. "We should leave her to walk back on her own," Tog grumbled.

"You know she'd never make it," Hiro said. "Besides, she'd grumble about 'negligent dragons' the entire way." He threw a glance over his shoulder at Anna, who was digging in her bag, but turned back to Tog. "Maybe you should head directly to Rakgar now. I'll take her home by myself then follow you. I'll only be a day behind you."

Tog lifted his head to level one eye at Hiro. He gazed past him toward the princess then back at his friend. "I'll be honest with you, Hiro," he sighed, "I don't trust you with her."

Hiro's jaw loosened, but he managed to keep it from dropping. "You really think I would eat her?"

Tog snorted and settled his head back on his claws. "Hardly."

Hiro knew what he meant, but couldn't believe how sensitive his best friend could be to his own feelings. What twisted hold did this little human have on him if it was obvious to others?

"Everything okay?" Anna stepped between the two beasts with her hand on Hiro's side.

Hiro curled onto the ground. "Fine," he grumbled.

"We were just wondering," Tog lifted his head, "how you learned of the dragons' intelligence?"

"I told you back in your cave," she said, sitting on the ground with her back against Hiro's side. "My father told me before he died."

"Yes, I know." Tog shifted his shoulder so he could look at her. "It's a royal secret. But wouldn't that mean your brother, King Philip, knows it as well?"

Anna nodded. "Normally it would, but my father told me in a rare moment when he was conscious and Philip wasn't present. I'm sure he never told Philip."

"Why didn't you tell him?" Hiro asked her.

She shrugged. "To be honest, I had a hard time believing it myself."

"Apparently you believed him enough to talk to me, trust me and trick Tog." Hiro gestured toward Tog with his three-taloned claw.

"Well, you were the real test." She looked up at him. "If you had done anything different, I wouldn't be here to worry about the results."

"But," Tog asked again, "why didn't you tell Philip this royal secret once you knew it to be true?"

Anna jerked her shoulders again. "I doubt he would believe me. Then or now. He doesn't have much faith in me, anyway."

Tog snorted. "I never thought I would see the day when I would agree with a human." He put his head down again. "Especially that human."

Anna pulled herself to her feet and walked toward a thick clump of trees. "I'll be back in a minute."

"Be careful," Hiro said after her.

"But not too careful," Tog added. He watched her go before swiveling his head toward Hiro. "How can we possibly trust a woman whose own kin doesn't trust her?"

"I have no reason not to trust her," he answered. "She's more trustworthy than faeries."

"Faeries?" Tog struggled to keep his voice low. "Faeries have hundreds of years' worth of trust built with the dragons. Shampy didn't lie to us. Everything she said has been true. I know Kradik and Ortym were liars at the best of times, but you can't blame an entire race on the actions of one—or two."

Hiro sighed. "Tog, I know you're trying to help me."

"But?"

Hiro checked to make sure Anna was far enough away not to hear them before continuing. "But I've never told you—in fact, I've never told anyone about Jarek."

"Jarek?" Tog pulled his head back. "What about the farmer?"

"Jarek came to visit me while I was prisoner in Philip's castle."

"More abuse made you trust humans?"

"No," Hiro shook his head. He had never put these thoughts into words before. "He didn't abuse me like the others did."

"So?"

"So," Hiro rolled his shoulder, "he didn't hurt me at all. He just walked by, staring at me." He shook his head again, but he couldn't remove the look of the human's eyes from his mind. "He could have persecuted me more than the others did. I invaded his territory. I probably frightened his mate. He was the only human there with any right to lash out at me. His abuse would have made sense, but he didn't do anything. He only stared at me."

"And this means what?" Tog asked.

"I think…" Hiro hesitated, "it felt like…"

"Like what?"

"Like he had come to forgive me."

"Is a human capable of forgiveness?"

"I don't know." Tog turned his head away again, but Hiro inched closer. "Think about it, Tog, if no two dragons are alike, why should any other species be different?"

Tog whipped his head back with teeth bared. "You're comparing dragons and humans now?"

"Milah and Mitashio are complete opposites of you and me," Hiro pressed, "but they aren't even much alike themselves. Milah is the one always lashing his tongue about, while Mitashio silently follows him."

"Two poor excuses for dragons." Tog's top lip pulled back even tighter.

"But if they can be so different from each other and from us," Hiro said, "why can't two humans like Jarek and Philip be different from each other? If one human can act civilized, perhaps there are more who can. You know there are rumors of other dragons believing the humans capable of knowing our secret."

"Blasphemy."

"Anna has proven at least one human can handle it." Hiro laid his head on the ground with a thump. "Perhaps Jarek as well."

Tog leveled his head at his friend. "You see logic where there is none. Don't be fooled by actions that appear honorable. Be careful in whom you put your trust, Hiro."

21

TRAP

While the trio waited they noticed a faint glimmer of moonlight seeping through the high, soft clouds. The rains of fall shifted to an uncommon brume, making even the night seem eerie.

"We'll have to walk over the mountains," Tog said, looking into the diffused moonlight in the clouds. "We can't fly through this, either." He pursed his lips at Hiro. "Perhaps she'd be safer if we let her walk."

Hiro lifted Anna with one claw and slid her onto his back. "You know we can cover more ground than her spindly little legs." Anna clicked her tongue at him, but he continued addressing Tog. "If she's in the elements it could be just as dangerous. I'll just take her to the other side of the mountains. You needn't come with us."

He set off at a trot toward the dark shapes of the mountains looming in front of them. Tog grumbled about it being a bad idea, but followed. Anna clung to Hiro's long neck with her arms and tucked her feet and lower legs under his wings.

They hiked in silence, which Tog insisted upon. At first Hiro didn't pay much attention to their surroundings. The trees shrank as they ranged further from the Black Forest. They passed a few open spaces and the land slanted steadily upward. Anna's death grip even loosened over time. When the land began to slope down, both dragons halted at the same time.

Hiro could feel the question in Anna's shifting from side to side on his back. He thought she must be looking around to see why they stopped. But Hiro and Tog both locked their eyes on a ridgeline of boulders to their right.

They stretched from the cleave in the two mountains and wrapped around the far side of the southernmost hill. The jumble of rocks wasn't large or intimidating, but the spread made a perfect hiding place. Although not impassable, the dragons were loath to step beside them.

Hiro stared into Tog's eye and jerked his chin at him to communicate wordlessly. *What do you want to do?*

Tog jerked his chin back at him, and pushed his nose ahead with a slight curve as if skirting the bottom of the rocks would help. *You should go through, around the bottom.*

Hiro jabbed his chin at Tog, snapping his jaws together, with a question in his eye. *And you?*

Tog swiped his head around in a curve in the opposite direction. *I'll go around, over the top.*

Hiro dipped his head to his friend and started to set off, but stopped when he heard Tog's low growl. Tog bared his fangs at Anna. She didn't need a translation. She immediately threw one leg over Hiro's back to slide down the other side, away from Tog.

"Where should I go?" Barely breathing the words in the empty darkness, it still seemed as if she shouted.

Hiro looked straight ahead, but bunched his neck to the side to whisper next to her. "Can you pick your way over those stones?"

She nodded. "I think so."

Without a second glance, Hiro crawled over the uneven ground in front of him. He crossed Anna's path to crawl toward where the two mountains met. He caught a glimpse of Tog scaling the mountainside to the north. Hiro had the shortest path, so he paused to watch Anna as she walked carefully toward the boulders.

While he watched, he listened to his surroundings since he had crawled in upwind. Rain dripping from the leaves made the most annoying thrumming sound. But somewhere beneath the noise of the forest was the muffled sound of human hearts beating. It was so faint that he couldn't be certain how close they were or how many, but he knew they waited for him.

Bunching his legs beneath him, he summoned the fire in his belly. He couldn't gain the sky through the trees, and jumping from the rocks would expose his wings, making it even easier for something to take him down. Instead he flung himself through the trees to try to get as far as possible beyond the boulders.

Multiple arrows assailed him first. Four pinched under his scales. A burst of red fire lit the sky directly over him, but it hadn't come from a dragon. The humans must be signaling each other—which meant that more would come.

He kept his wings tight against his side. They would be his only escape. He whirled to face his attackers. At least ten human men crouched behind the boulders. He loosed his fire to sweep over them, but they easily ducked between the rocks.

When his flame died down, half of the men stood up and pointed heavy crossbows at him. Before he could move, three dragon-killers buried deep under his scales. Unlike the arrows, they made his ribs feel as if they were exploding. Hiro's roar cut short from the pain. He didn't have time to counter as the other half of the men rushed him with spears.

They all wore the blue tunics of the Noble Kingdom and so must have been trained to fight. They stabbed toward the dragon with their long spears, but danced away when he tried to swing a claw at them.

As the spearmen kept him busy, the other men set aside their crossbows to pull out their swords. Hiro saw no chains this time. These men had no misguided notions to capture any dragons. They wanted ash.

Hiro engaged a spearman intent on piercing his fleshy leg joint. Another man with a sword launched himself from a boulder into the air. When the swordsman came down short of Hiro, he thought the man had simply misjudged the distance. Then he felt the cold slice of pain rip through the length of his wing. He knew he must get away, but he certainly couldn't fly now.

He swung his head away from the rocks and felt the sting of a blade across his back leg. Another struck again at almost the same spot before he could drag himself away. The deep cuts made his leg fight to obey his commands.

Hiro limped through the trees with the men close behind him. He struggled for breath and footing as he first swept up the side of the south mountain, then back down. He roared again as one of the men sliced into the underside of his tail.

"The back leg is weak!" one of the men yelled. "Aim for it!"

Two spears bounced off the lower part of his leg as he continued faltering down the mountain. A third buried deep into the gash. Hiro roared again as he rolled over himself down the slope.

"We've almost got it, men!" someone yelled.

Having gained a small amount of distance between him and the men, Hiro stopped to reach his head around to his back leg. He didn't know how it hadn't already turned to embers. The gash felt as deep as when Shampy had dug for marrow. His leg was all but incapacitated, but he ripped the spear free anyway.

He roared again, but didn't have time to do anything else. Three men jumped on top of him with swords in hand. Hiro was on his side with his back against two trees, unable to roll away from them. The men hacked at his scales like they were felling a tree. Hiro swiped one of them off, but the other two twisted their swords to poise them in a killing position over his breast.

Before their death swords could fall, another human man sailed through the air, screaming and knocked one of the men from Hiro's chest to the ground. The pile of creatures turned in surprise from the interruption. The other human's sword jolted from his hand.

The gray dragon ran through the forest toward them with a snarl on his face. He stomped on one of the men behind them, spilling head contents into the soil.

"Two?" the man atop Hiro exclaimed. "Two dragons?"

But neither man said anything more. Hiro closed his eyes as flame washed over all three of them. The remains of the humans melted to the ground. The arrow remains burned from Hiro's chest.

Once the flame ceased, Tog slipped his neck under Hiro's front leg. "Thanks for taking all the attention off of me."

"Next time, you're the bait." Hiro cringed with pain when he spoke.

"More men are coming," Tog lifted Hiro to his feet. "We need to grab Anna."

The two dragons hobbled away from the torched trees. Further down the mountainside, Anna stood staring into the trees, waiting for them. Tog dropped Hiro in a heap on the ground next to her, but turned immediately to face the direction they'd come.

"I saw another camp from the ridge," Tog said, watching the darkness around them. "We haven't much time, but we should be able to stay ahead of them."

"We've reached the other side of the mountain," Anna said, surveying Hiro's wounds. "I can go on alone from here."

"And make him go back through all that?" Tog snapped at her, indicating the ambush they'd just blustered through.

"I can make it," Hiro moaned, but as he tried to get his claws under him, all four legs buckled from pain.

"You can't fly. You can barely stand." Tog faced Hiro full on. "You need to heal before you can go anywhere, and if we stay here more humans will find us."

Anna looked around bewildered and then whipped her head to face them. "The Hamees."

"The what?" Tog snapped at her again.

"Jarek, the farmer who helped me a few months ago, he's part of the Hamees community," she clarified. "They swear to take in anyone who needs help."

"Humans?" Tog growled.

"Yes, but they'll help us. They helped me before; I'm sure they can help us now."

"They won't hide two dragons," Hiro moaned. "I don't care what they swear."

"Maybe not two," she hemmed, "but one….and severely injured at that…they might."

"Might?" Tog snarled.

"What other choice do we have?" Anna's hands poised over Hiro's wounds, shaking. "They used cave-tipped bolts. They're used to hunt large animals, spreading within on impact." She looked back up at Tog. "He needs to get to a healer or majishun quickly or…he might die."

After an acute hesitation, Hiro lifted his head. "Tog, the other humans coming, do they know there are two of us?"

Tog just growled.

"If you let them see you fly away, they might think they're safe or even follow you."

"It would at least give us some time," Anna added.

"You need to report to Rakgar, anyway," Hiro pressed further. "Bring back help if you can."

"We know how well that worked out last time." Tog shook his head slowly in frustration. The last time he asked Rakgar to send help for Hiro, he was forced to stay back and contemplate Hiro's death.

Tog looked at Hiro. He eyed his heavy wounds. He stared into the trees behind them. He grimaced at Anna and stared into the trees again.

"Tog," Hiro whispered, "we don't have much time."

"Fine." He grabbed Anna around the waist and threw her none-too-gently on his back.

"Ow!" she squeaked at the ridges running down his spine.

"Quiet, human." Tog leaned over Hiro. "Hold onto me. I'll fly you away from here to cover your tracks."

Hiro struggled to wrap his legs around Tog. His back right leg hung lifeless as did the tip of his tail. He grumbled low as Tog lifted off and scratched his wings against the tree branches, but finally got above them. Tog dragged Hiro through the trees with whispered apologies before he finally set all three down at the base of the mountain.

Anna jumped from his back without being asked. "Hiro, can you walk a little way?"

Hiro rolled onto his stomach and pushed himself up with his three barely stable legs. "I'll have to try, won't I?" Looking around, he recognized the area. He'd flown over this pass only a few months before. Jarek's little village was down the path to his left.

"Make sure to get him some flarote," Tog said while searching the sky.

"Like Shampy gave him?" Anna asked.

"Yes," he grunted and leveled his head at Hiro. "I hope these Hamees drown you."

"Clear skies to you as well!"

Suddenly, Tog lashed out his claws and wrapped them around Anna's arms, pinning them to her sides. He drew her directly in front of his face and allowed flame to tickle his tongue. "If anything should happen to him, human, I'll hunt you down and peel the skin from your bones."

"I would deserve no less," she answered. She held his gaze for a moment before he placed her back on the ground.

Hiro coughed. Tog snarled while eyeing his best friend and his little human companion, then launched himself back into the night sky.

"Come on," Hiro offered his claw to Anna.

"I will not." She clenched her fists with stiff arms at her sides. "You can barely carry yourself."

"We can't leave our tracks side-by-side."

"We won't." She pointed down the pathway. "I'll run this way into the village. You'll have to sneak in from the outside. Wait for me behind Jarek's barn." She put her hands on her hips. "You do know where Jarek's barn is, don't you?"

With a little effort, Hiro shoved her away from him with one claw. "Get moving."

22

HAMEES HELP

Hiro lay still behind the barn. The last time he was here, the beasts inside had raised a ruckus. This time they must have sensed his weakness. He could hear them snuffling on the other side of the wall, but other than the occasional yelp, they held their peace.

Even with a lame leg, his straighter course caused him to arrive ahead of Anna. She had to weed her way down the path and through the village with no light or help, but still she arrived just after him. He listened to her urgent conversation with Jarek.

"Please, Jarek," she pleaded as soon as the door opened, "we need help."

"We?" the farmer stood in his doorway at the back of his home. His wife hadn't come to the door.

"Yes," she said, "my friend is hurt badly. We just need somewhere to stay until he heals."

"But Kingstor is less than half a day's ride from here."

Hiro could hear movement and thought Anna must have been shaking her head. "He won't make it."

He heard more rustling. "Well, then, bring your friend in."

"No, no," she stammered, "he'll have to stay in the barn."

"The friend of a princess staying in a barn?"

"You'll understand when you meet him. Please."

"Alright." Hiro could hear more movement like Jarek was pulling cloth around his shoulders. "You know our oaths, Anna. I'll do whatever I can."

He could hear four feet sloshing over the soggy ground toward him. "This might be more than your oath requires," Anna said. The footsteps stopped.

"What's going on, Anna?"

"Just please believe me when I say that you and your family are perfectly safe," she told him. "I promise you."

"I believe you."

"Jarek," Anna turned the corner to face Hiro, "let me introduce you to Hiro."

When Jarek followed her, the color drained from his face. Hiro lay on the ground against the barn wall with ash dripping from his chest and leg. He could barely raise his head far enough to meet the eyes of the man, but he was impressed that Jarek didn't run screaming. He didn't even take a single step backward.

"Hiro?" the man said. "That's his name?" He actually squatted in front of him to look into his eye.

"Yes," Anna answered behind him.

"You gave him that name?" Jarek stroked Hiro's snout with a shaky hand. Hiro didn't flinch.

"Yes." Jarek missed Anna's face scrunching as she lied.

Finally Jarek turned his widened eyes back to the princess, who smoothed her expression. "How do you come to be in company with a dragon?"

Hiro's eyes narrowed at Anna. *Don't you dare,* he thought.

"He's…kind of…my…pet."

She dared.

Hiro's lip twisted with anger, but he stilled it when Jarek turned back to look at him. Behind the farmer, Anna shrugged her shoulders helplessly.

"Is this the same dragon the king is looking for?" Jarek asked. Hiro admired how he got right to the tip of the claw.

"Yes."

"I understand," Jarek said with a smile. "This dragon was following you when you showed up here." Anna's face paled. "The king found it, it escaped and has been trying to get back to you ever since."

Anna took a breath. "Yes, yes, exactly."

"Why don't you just explain it to him?" Jarek stood up to look at her. "He's your brother, after all, and you have a tame dragon."

Hiro's lip twisted again. *Tame, indeed.*

"You've seen how Philip treats dragons, Jarek," she told him. "He can never know. He'll kill him."

Jarek looked into the now-misting rain. "How long do you need to stay?"

"Maybe two days."

After a moment, the farmer nodded. "Bring him into the barn. We can help him dig his way under the hay to stay out of sight and keep warm."

Anna flung her arms around the man. "Thank you, Jarek. May your God bless you abundantly!"

Once free from her hold, Jarek patted her arm and walked around to the large doors on the side of the structure. Unlatching them, he swung one out and pulled it far enough away from the building to create an opening that fit most of Hiro's girth. He pushed the other door into the building so that Hiro only had to round a small corner to follow the humans inside.

"Come, Hiro," Anna said for Jarek's benefit, and Hiro glared at her.

Hiro was immediately relieved once he was inside. The cold and wet outdoors had sapped his strength. Careful to avoid his injuries, he curled on the floor looking around. A small loft with bales of hay covered half of the barn's interior. Two dogs and a horse were tethered to a wall just inside the doors. On the other side of the barn were some large and small wooden crates and barrels alongside tools with long, wooden handles and sharp, distorted metal ends. A large mound of hay took up the rest of the barn and filled the side closest to Jarek's home.

One of the dogs crept up to Hiro with its nose down. Hiro's first impulse was to roar at the smelly creature, but he realized he would have to remain in this space with them. He allowed the animal to sniff him all over, even the gaping holes in his chest, but the animal was smarter than he thought. It didn't attempt to lick the wounds.

Now I'm impressed with both humans' behavior and their pets', he thought. *I suppose I'll eat from a dish next.*

Hiro grumbled and shifted, scaring away the animal again.

"With the dragon in this condition at least the dogs will keep quiet while he's here," Jarek said, swinging the doors shut. "I won't have to take them out in this rain and draw any attention we don't want." He plucked one of the tools from the wall. "Can he dig?"

"I'm not sure," Anna said. She chose another tool. "I'm sure he'll try. He's stubborn like that."

Jarek walked to the far edge of the hay. "Less noticeable over here," he said, shoving the tool into the earth next to it. Again and again he shifted dirt away from the edge. Anna used her tool to scrape away the dirt and hay. "You needn't do that," Jarek said without looking at her.

She ignored him and continued her effort. "I told you," she answered, "I was raised to work."

Hiro knew it might be all night and all the next day before they dug anything close to large enough for him to hide in. He dragged himself over to where they dug.

A subservient pet would ask permission, he thought. So he nudged Anna with his head.

"Yes, Hiro," she huffed as she continued to scrape, "dig."

With one claw he scooped at the ground. Jarek's pile instantly doubled.

"That will certainly help," Jarek mumbled.

Hiro took turns with Jarek digging while Anna pulled the hay away. After a while, they'd made a large trench halfway under the pile of hay. Finally, Hiro pushed past Jarek into the trench and didn't come back out. He dug further into the pile, scratching the mixture of dirt and hay out of his way. Behind him, Anna and Jarek started shoveling the dirt and hay over his back half. Eventually his head stuck out the other side. When they were finished his body lay in a trench of dirt with his back pressed against the wall of the barn, burying him under the thickest part of the haystack.

"I think that will do," Jarek said inspecting Hiro's view from the doorway.

Anna lifted her tool onto her shoulder. "We'll need to cover his tracks outside," she said, stepping toward the door.

"I'll do that." Jarek took the tool from her hand. "First I'll take you inside for Boorda to attend you."

"But..." Anna started.

Jarek cut her off. "She would insist, as do I." He pushed the door open for her.

Anna glanced back at Hiro. "I don't think we should mention Hiro."

"Nor do I," Jarek agreed. "It would only frighten her."

Anna nodded and slipped out of the barn with him. Hiro could hear them outside. "We need to find some flarote for him."

"Flarote?" Jarek asked. "Why?"

"Well," Anna said, "it helps heal animals, doesn't it?"

"I suppose I've seen the doctor use it on some animals."

"I think we should try it," Anna insisted.

"It's rather scarce this time of year, but I'll see what I can do."

Hiro heard the two humans enter the house. He could still make out the muffled sound of shuffling feet. "Anna?" Another woman's voice whispered. "I mean, Princess Anna?"

"'Anna' is fine," she answered. "It's nice to see you, Boorda. I'm sorry to impose this way."

"Don't worry about that, my dear. Go upstairs and undress, I'll bring you some hot water to wash." Hiro heard footsteps on the stairs, but then they stopped.

"Boorda," Anna said, "I know this is a lot to ask, but I'd rather no one know that I'm here. If anyone comes asking, could you not mention it?"

"I'll do what I can," Boorda answered. Hiro could hear the hesitation in her voice. "But I won't go against my oath of honesty. You know that."

"I know," Anna said, "but I'll thank you for trying, anyway."

Anna's footsteps continued up the stairs, but his attention was drawn back to the humans at the bottom. "Jarek," the woman addressed her husband, "it's almost dawn. Why are you so filthy? What's going on?"

Hiro heard Jarek heave a sigh. He could imagine the man staring into the eyes of his wife with the same unwavering gaze that still haunted him. "Someday, Boorda." Then silence.

Jarek came back outside. He retrieved the tools from the side of the barn where he'd laid them and took the one Anna had been using behind the barn. Hiro listened as he scratched at the ground outside. While Jarek worked, Hiro could only barely hear the women talking inside. But what Jarek said to her must have been some kind of signal because she didn't question Anna, not once, about her presence.

While Anna was fed and cleansed inside, Hiro snuggled under his haystack. The ground under him soon warmed to his body temperature to make the situation quite comfortable. He even considered bringing some hay back to his cave in the Rock Clouds. Should he return.

He listened as Jarek scraped at the ground outside. The man was obviously a hard worker. Hiro thought it must have added to his workload to ensure Hiro's tracks were covered. But Hiro knew the man would do it to protect himself from the consequences of others knowing about the dragon's presence. He probably also wanted to prevent his mate from being frightened. But as the man worked further and further into the trees and beyond, Hiro wondered why he was trying so hard to help them. Could a human possibly be so kind and concerned? His actions had already exceeded any dragon's expectations.

23

OVERSEER

Hiro awoke cuddled under his hay blanket to fast, heavy footfalls outside the barn. The sun was brightening the sky in a rarely seen misty morning of fall. Jarek threw the barn door open with his tool in hand. Closing the door behind him, he turned to Hiro. "The King's Guard is coming." Hiro tried not to react to the words. How had they been found so soon? "We have to hide your head. Just in case." He stepped lightly toward Hiro. "Easy now. We have to cover you." Jarek waved his arms as if using them to cover Hiro. "Cover—" he said louder, "—hide!"

Hiro thought he'd better indicate that he understood, to some extent, what Jarek was trying to say. He pulled his head deeper into the haystack. "Yes," Jarek said, "hide. You must be used to hearing that command from Anna."

Hiro wriggled his head and tail, tucking them into his body. He wrapped his tail over his body almost the length of him, wincing every time the broken tip snagged on the hay. His head, he couldn't do as much with. He tucked it up against the side of the wall while Jarek piled more hay on top of it. He squeezed his eyes shut as the hay fell on him, but when he heard the farmer moving one of the crates to put in front of his head, he lifted his eyelids. Even with the hay partially blocking his vision, he could see between the slats of the barn into the village and the back of Jarek's house.

Hiro listened as Jarek filled one bucket with liquid from the barrels and another with a few hard things from a crate. They smelled like eggs. Hiro watched as the man carried the buckets into his house seeming as casually as he could manage.

Once Jarek was inside Hiro heard him call to Boorda. "The Guard is coming to the village," he told her. As he said it, Hiro heard hooves pounding on the road into the village. "No matter what happens," the man told his wife, "stay inside. Inform Anna, but keep her inside, too. Do you understand?"

As the horses beat their rhythm down the sodden path, more villagers appeared in the streets. After pausing behind the corner of his house to listen to the Guard's approach, Jarek stepped out alongside the others.

"Captain!" Jarek exclaimed with confidence over the babble of voices, as if he had spoken to the guards before. "You said you needed to speak to the leader of our village. That would be Rika, a good friend of mine."

Jarek disappeared around the front of his house as he gestured to someone Hiro couldn't see. The four men on horses dismounted and the one in front placed a fist over his heart with his thumb facing his chest as if he was stabbing himself. "I am Captain Murzod," he stated.

"I'm Rika." Hiro had heard the man's deep voice a few months previous. He hadn't forgotten it. "How can I serve the King's Guard?"

"We tracked a dragon into the area overnight," Murzod announced to the shocked response of the crowd. He paused, and with Hiro's sharp eyes he saw the slightest twist of an evil grin on his face. Murzod enjoyed scaring people.

After the murmur died down, Rika spoke up. "No one has seen a dragon in this area for many years."

Murzod pulled a paper from a saddle bag, flipped it over and placed it back in the bag. "My report," he addressed Rika again, "says your village reported the presence of a dragon not three months ago."

"Yes," Rika answered. Hiro could hear his boots shifting in the mud just on the other side of Jarek's house. "One of our farmers found footprints, but that was all. No one saw anything else."

Murzod turned his gaze back to where Jarek had gone behind the house. "Would that be the 'early riser' I met in the woods?" he asked with a sneer.

"Matter of fact," Hiro heard Jarek say, "it was me. I found claw marks as big as my dogs behind my home."

Murzod swept the cowl of his cloak from his head. He had thin black and white hair. The skin around his eyes pinched together. It might have been from excessive laughter, but Hiro thought it more likely that he squinted a lot. Murzod stepped between the buildings where Jarek had come from when he greeted them, and stared at the barn. Hiro froze. "Behind your home, you say?"

Rika and Jarek rounded the corner behind Murzod. "Yes, sir," Jarek replied quietly. Hiro saw a brief glance between the two men.

"We set up a watch that very night," Rika offered, "but no one actually saw a dragon."

The captain stared carefully at the home's surroundings for a few minutes. Luckily he stood with his back to the house when Anna appeared in one of the windows. A blanket wrapped her shoulders and her hair was matted to one side, but her eyes were as fierce as ever. When Murzod turned back to face the villagers, whose numbers continued to grow, Anna disappeared without a split second to spare.

Murzod's eyes bore into Jarek. Hiro's heart throbbed in his chest against the dirt floor. "Did you see a dragon?"

Hiro recalled the oath of honesty Boorda spoke of. Did this oath pertain to Jarek? Must he tell the captain of Hiro's presence or risk the wrath of the Guard and the gods? What kind of human was this simple farmer in whom Anna put her trust?

"No," Jarek answered without blinking, "I never saw a dragon until I visited the one the king held captive."

Murzod stepped close enough for Jarek to feel his breath on his face, which Hiro was sure he did. "Have you seen one within the past day?"

Again Jarek didn't blink. "No."

Murzod's and Jarek's eyes remained locked in a battle of wills. Finally, Murzod walked past him to address the villagers. "Has anyone seen any dragon today or yesterday?" he called out.

Many heads shook "No." Mothers clutched small children to them. Hiro thought he could even see the little boy Harry being contained by his mother. He felt better knowing the child had survived his disobedience of the past season.

"Perhaps the captain is unfamiliar," Rika spoke with a degree of hesitation, "but we're Hamees. We take very serious oaths of honesty and integrity in our religion. If no one here says they've seen a dragon, then no one has seen a dragon. I'd bet my life on it."

Murzod gave him a half-grin. "Would you?" Murzod pointed to Jarek. "Would you bet his?"

Rika swallowed. Hiro would have been shocked if the whole village didn't hear that swallow.

Murzod turned back to the barn. "What does this building contain?" He pointed directly where Hiro was hidden.

"Hay," Jarek shrugged.

Murzod gestured to the other guards with him. "We'll need to search it." The men handed the reins of their horses to a couple of villagers and tromped past the people to the barn. "Open it," Murzod demanded.

Hiro's injuries throbbed as his heart tumbled in his chest. He attempted to still his breathing, hoping he could trust the hay covering him. He could barely see the men from the corner of his eye as they stood in the doorway behind Jarek. Rika stood behind the soldiers, watching.

"Impressive stock for one horse," Murzod said, taking in the barn and its occupants.

Jarek's jaw worked a little. "I store hay for the entire village. This has to last the rest of the year until harvest."

Murzod stepped over to the wall and picked up one of the tools from it. Returning to the group of men, he handed it to one of the guards. The tool had three long, sharp tines. "Search the pile. You," he pointed to the other guards, "use your swords."

Hiro couldn't see the men as they approached so he tried to focus on the ones that stayed behind. Rika watched Jarek, but Jarek wouldn't meet his eye. When Murzod stepped back to watch his men work, Jarek asked, "Would they like some help?"

Hiro felt the men step onto the pile of hay. They weren't farmers, so they obviously didn't know how to use the tools the way Jarek did, but why would the farmer offer to help them?

Murzod folded his arms across his chest. "I'm sure they can manage."

The guards scraped and scratched at the great pile in front of them. *How long will they dig?* Hiro wondered. *How soon before they find me?*

"Is this really necessary?" Rika asked. "No one is stupid enough to hide a dragon in a pile of hay. Especially when this hay is our livelihood."

Hiro couldn't see what the men atop him were doing, but Murzod indicated the pile. "Just stab it," he ordered. "The King's Guard are charged with keeping the people of this country safe," he told the village men. "We wouldn't want a dragon getting into your barn and endangering you, now would we?" Turning back to the men, he ordered, "All the way down to the dirt. We don't want to miss anything."

That's when the first sword struck his tail. Hiro struggled to remain still, but his eyes popped open with the pain. Then the second sword pierced his back leg. His other wounds had been warming but now all of them simultaneously burst with freezing pain. Another stabbing pain shot into his side. Another exploded in his belly.

Hiro pinched his eyes shut and focused on holding still. Ten icy wounds gaped. Eleven. Twelve. Finally one sword sliced through the top of his neck and landed with a thud against the barn wall.

"I think we're just striking dirt, sir," one of the men standing on the haystack announced.

Thank Shurka for that man! Hiro thought.

He took a slow breath, considering the humans standing silently around him waiting for orders. When the immediate pain subsided and he could finally open his eyes, he did so only a fraction. Murzod stood glaring at the upended contents of the barn with his hand on his sword hilt. Finally, he nodded his head.

The men stepped down from the haystack and Hiro could see Jarek breathing again. He couldn't feel the same sense of relief; he couldn't even take the same breath without pain.

As the men walked out of the barn past Murzod, he thrust his hand out and grabbed one of the guards' arms. "Bring me a torch," he murmured, still staring into the barn.

Rika's and Jarek's wide eyes met again. "Would you like to search elsewhere?" Rika offered. "Our village has nothing to hide from the King's Guard."

Jarek's breathing increased as he stared at the back of Murzod's head. Murzod stared into the barn.

Minutes passed. No one spoke. Hiro could have sworn he saw hatred burn in Murzod's eyes.

Eventually, a man with the torch approached from the direction of the village. Before Murzod accepted it, he faced the village leader.

"Please, sir," Rika pleaded, "remember our oaths. We would never hide anything from you."

Murzod took the torch and nodded his head at the farmers. "Restrain them."

"No!" the village men yelled, but the guards held them while Murzod tossed the torch into the barn. "You can't do this! We won't survive! Please!"

Their cries muffled as Murzod heaved the door shut behind him. Murzod hefted a substantial piece of wood across the doors to block the way.

Inside the barn the flames licked the bottom of the haystack. The humans screamed outside while Jarek's horse and two dogs kicked up a racket inside. Because the ground was soggy from the constant rain, the fire didn't spread fast, but Hiro knew it would eventually engulf the entire barn. Rain or not.

Hiro could see Anna and Boorda with their arms wrapped around each other staring out the upper window of the house. Tears streaked their faces. He heard a shallow threat shouted to the startled villagers watching the scene before the guards released the men and rode away from the village.

Hiro felt the flames next to his head. He watched as Rika began to bark orders at the men in the village. Many of them disappeared to fetch buckets. The women sobbed into aprons and blankets. A few children with bewildered looks on their faces cried.

Hiro had planned to let the hay burn. The heat would feel good, and the rubble would land on him and continue to hide him as well. He knew he shouldn't get involved, anyway. Until the young boy—Harry—stepped out of the crowd. No tears ran down his face. He just looked confused as he watched smoke seep from the barn.

Hiro gave a low snort. What kind of hold did that small human have on him? He really did resemble the young child in Eoaa. With a grunt, he pulled his head from the hay Jarek had piled on him and shoved it straight into the fire at his side. Only a small portion of the haystack was alight, but the amount of smoke billowing to the ceiling made it seem much more disastrous.

Hiro pulled in a deep draft of flames with his nose. It was simple fire, but it smelled good. Earthy. He pulled harder at the flames with his mouth and nose as they fought to burn stronger. The warmth made it easier to breathe deep against his wounds and soothe them. One more pull on the flames and they sputtered out. Hiro licked his lips from the taste. It was similar to horse, when he thought about it. He barely shoved his head back behind the crate before one of the villagers pulled the door open.

The man stopped short, water from the bucket in his arms sloshing over his boots. Another man stopped abruptly behind him, sloshing more water over his back, but the first man didn't seem to notice. The two men stared wide-eyed at the non-existent fire.

Hiro watched the humans stumble over each other in their haste to fight the fire they thought was burning. Soon the crowd gathered and the barn doors were opened wide enough for all to see inside.

"It's a miracle," someone whispered when Jarek and Rika appeared in the awe-struck crowd.

One by one, villagers fell to their knees. Men, women and children bowed their heads. Rika said a few words of thanks to someone unseen—apparently in the sky for all the times he looked up—for sparing their village. Soon all the humans gabbled and slapped Jarek on the back. Even Rika smiled and laughed at the "fools for guards."

"Our God protects the innocent as we try to be like Him," he said to Jarek and the others. Jarek nodded, but stared at the crate in front of Hiro's head without returning any of the gestures.

24

RESPONSIBILITY

"They take their oaths of honesty very seriously," Anna told Hiro as she inspected the damage to his tail from behind the haystack. She came down to check on him as soon as the crowd cleared. "For Jarek to lie to the Guard about not seeing a dragon must have been extremely difficult."

Hiro flinched as she touched his tail. "Why would he do that? He owes us nothing."

"Well," Anna said, coming around to face him. "The Hamees also take oaths to care for anyone who needs help. That's the reason he took me in when he first found me. These oaths are the reason I hoped he would help us."

Hiro pulled his tail back under the hay. "That would present a difficult problem if the two oaths counteracted each other."

Anna pushed the hay away from in front of Hiro. He squeezed out from under it so she could see the fresh wounds in his side. "It would be a difficult choice for anyone to make, but Jarek did and let's be grateful he chose us."

"Do other humans have to make such decisions, too?" He growled as she poked a sword wound.

"This one is shallower than where the bolts hit." She shook her head and sat up straight. "Other humans don't live by such strict laws as the Hamees."

Hiro cocked his head at her. "Oh?"

"The Hamees are different and they're often harshly judged because of those differences." She moved closer to sit on the crate that hid his head. "The Hamees believe in one almighty God rather than the Seven High Gods of Avonoa, but their God demands much more. They are supposed to be kind, honest, pure, faithful, charitable and much more. At the same time, even with all these strictures, they claim their way of life is easier and happier." She smiled an odd peaceful grin, a look Hiro hadn't seen on her before. "They seem very happy in their way. Sometimes I wish—"

"Someone's coming," Hiro whispered. He lifted his head behind the crate again, just in case.

"I got some flarote," Jarek said, opening the barn door. Hiro pulled his head out again when Anna called him. "I told the doc I thought my horse might need it after all this. He had some left."

Anna took the little red bulb from him. "Thank you. I'll make sure you're compensated—for everything."

Jarek settled on an overturned bucket by the door as Anna ministered to Hiro. "You know, you could have told us a tame dragon might come looking for you the first time we met."

Hiro scowled at her with one eye. She rolled her eyes back at him before addressing Jarek. "Would you have believed me?"

"Once I saw the claw marks in the ground, I would have."

She dropped the bulb onto Hiro's outstretched tongue. It melted before he could even close his mouth. The warmth spread through him faster than he expected. The cold in his injuries gradually began to tingle.

"What would Boorda say if she knew?" Anna asked. "I thought it might scare her."

"She's tougher than you might think." Jarek stood up. "Although she's not fond of the idea of me spending a lot of time with another woman."

"Your oath of chastity?" Anna guessed.

Jarek nodded. "My personal oath not to make my wife angry."

Anna smiled. "You'd better go, then." But Anna called to him before he left. "Why?" she asked when he faced her again. "You took an oath of honesty. Why did you lie for us?"

Jarek scrubbed his hands through his hair before answering. "I also took an oath to help others, remember? We're taught that God understands when you have to choose between doing two good things." He shrugged his shoulders and squinted in the direction Murzod and the Guard had left the village. "If that captain seemed a reasonable fellow, I might've told him everything. But he found me just off the road as I was scratching away the last of the claw marks and I could tell as soon as I met his eye—that man is rotten as a year-old apple core."

Once Jarek was safely in the house, Hiro stretched and snuggled under the hay. "What did Jarek mean when he told his wife, 'Someday'?" The tingling in his wounds felt like snakes under his scales. But warm snakes, not icy.

Anna spread her skirts out on the hay next to Hiro's head. Jarek had removed the burnt hay earlier along with the frightened animals. "The Hamees use such a phrase in order to avoid deceiving one another. It means, 'I can't tell you everything, but I don't want to lie to you. I promise to tell you all, someday.'"

Hiro laid his head next to her. His eyelids seemed heavier than ever. "You should head back to Kingstor before you're missed."

Anna threw an arm behind her head. "I want to make sure you're well on your way to healing."

"I just need some rest." A dog barked outside in the village. "Perhaps one of those creatures for a snack."

"When was the last time you ate?" she asked as her own eyelids wilted.

"Let me sleep or I'll eat you."

———

Anna returned to the house later in the day. While Hiro slept in the barn, his tingling turned first to itching, then to burning. The warmth and comfort from the burning felt so good that he slept awhile longer after she'd gone inside. He woke briefly once to hear the humans inside discussing her presence in the village. Boorda never asked what was going on in the barn. She talked as if she knew Anna should be out there instead of inside. She even offered to bring her meals to the barn, but Anna politely refused.

When the sun began to slip behind the mountains, Anna came to visit Hiro one last time. Sidling through the barn doors, she said nothing. She sat by Hiro's head again and waited.

"I'll leave tonight," he finally said.

"I know." She wouldn't look at him.

"You were right." That raised her eyebrows into her hair. "These are good humans and they did help us," he said with a grin.

"Good humans?"

"We shouldn't endanger them any further."

"No," she shook her head, "you're right about that. But what will be done about the wraith?"

"You'll have to speak to your brother." As the sun disappeared, shadows hid her expression. "Try to convince him of the real danger. I'll try to convince Rakgar to allow me to come back and help you."

He saw her head whip toward him. "You would do that?"

"Not for you," he sniggered, "but these Hamees creatures lay between the wraith and the king. I'll try to repay them in my own way."

After a long silence, Anna asked, "What if Rakgar doesn't allow you to return?"

He didn't want to tell her just how indebted he felt to the Hamees and to Jarek, in particular. He certainly couldn't admit the lengths he might be willing to go to help them, so he stayed silent. "You still have the ribbon?" Anna nodded. "Then I'll leave some of my fire with you. Perhaps you can get Jarek and Rika to help you destroy the wraith. If your brother won't."

"Well," she stood up, "I suppose I've asked enough of you already." She stepped out of the barn to fetch a large branch. Upon returning she held it out to Hiro. "It's rather wet. The rain is picking up again."

"I'll manage," he muttered. Pulling his front claw out from under the haystack, he cradled the branch. First he bathed it in warm air. It steamed and fizzed in his claw. Then he directed hot flame at one end. Almost instantly, the tip of the branch burst with sparkling flame.

Anna lifted one end of the branch, holding it out in front of her. "Hiro," she spoke to the floor, "if I don't see you again—"

"—I'll be the happiest dragon in the history of Avonoa."

25

FIRE AND FAMILY

"Thank Khurta you're home safely, sister." Philip's scowl didn't match his words. He had received word of Anna's return and gone to call on her in her chambers. However, they'd met in the corridor. She had thrown a clean green cloak with a thick fur mantel over her, but her hair and dress weren't fit for a sewer. Philip wrinkled his nose at her. "What's happened to you?"

"I was just coming to see you," she told him. "I hope you weren't concerned for my safety."

"Anna, we haven't the men or the time to waste searching the mountains for you. And," he pointed to the implement in her hand, "what is that?"

She held it up for his inspection. "A lantern. I picked it up along the way. It has dragon fire in it."

"Why do you need dragon fire?" She opened her mouth, but he cut her off with a wave of his hand. "Never mind. Where have you been? And why do you keep disappearing?"

She lowered the lantern and pursed her lips. "Philip," she said, "you know I was raised in the freedom of the mountains. It's not something I can give up easily. Even in fall. Besides, I need to tell you about the dragon fire." She rattled the lantern for emphasis, but he waved it away again.

"I don't care, Anna." He clenched a fist to control himself. "You're a princess of Avonoa. You can't be seen in possession of dragon materials when we're practically at war with one."

"But Philip, it's—"

"Enough, Anna," he barked. "The people are beginning to wonder about your disappearances all the time. The faeries don't trust you enough to tell you anything and I don't know what to think of you. If you can't—"

"What do you mean the faeries don't trust me?" she interrupted. "Have you been plotting with them in my absence? Are they telling you I'm not who I say I am?"

"On the contrary," he kept his voice low as servants scuttled by, "they have said you are exactly who you say, but that's the reason they don't trust you. What am I supposed to make of it?"

Anna took note of the servants. "Why don't you accompany me to my chambers so I can get cleaned up, brother?" She turned back the way she'd come and Philip fell into step beside her, the lantern swinging between them. "Philip," she started in a gentler tone, "I am trying to help you. I have information about the creature coming to Kingstor."

"And where did you get this information?"

"From a faerie shaman."

He noticed she didn't specify the name or location of this shaman. "I have faeries enough advising me, Anna."

"But—"

"And they come from the Faerie Council," he continued, "I can't ignore their advice nor sway them from their plans. Believe me, I've tried."

"Plans?" Anna stopped to stare hard at Philip.

He ignored the break in her step and kept walking. When she caught up to him again, he continued. "Yes, Anna. Plans. The entire Faerie Council has chosen a most dangerous path and I'm forced to assist them."

"How can they—?"

"If I don't comply I'll have a possessed dragon, maybe more than one, at my face and thousands of faeries with powerful majik at my back." He stopped in front of her chamber doors.

For once, it took Anna a moment to compose a response. "Philip, if you would tell me what's going on, I could help you."

"The faeries made me swear not to divulge anything to you."

Anna stared at him in shock. Eventually, Philip dropped his gaze. Finally she spoke. "What can I do?"

He lifted his eyes to hers. "You can start acting like the princess you are."

"Tell me what to do." She straightened her back. "I want you to know you can trust me. Tell me what to do and I'll do it."

Philip paused to think. It was an idea he'd been toying with, something he knew must happen since he'd met Anna. He shifted on his feet as he grappled with his feelings. Finally he turned to face her. "The man you marry will be next in line for the throne." Her face went slack, but he forced himself to continue. "The duty of a princess of Avonoa is to marry—correctly."

"So," she huffed, "to earn your trust I must find a man to marry."

"No," Philip stiffened, "although not disappearing so often might help. It remains my duty to find a husband for you. A princess must marry the right man for the kingdom." He lifted the lantern from her hand, inspected it, then suddenly hammered the lever to extinguish the flame with a bang that echoed through the halls.

Anna flinched at the action before clenching her jaw and squaring her shoulders. "Well," she said, pushing past him to open the door to her rooms, "then you must find me a husband quickly." She turned long enough to stab him with her eyes. "I'm eager to prove my loyalty." She slammed the door behind her.

26

ASSENT

Hiro flew above the clouds all night. The fall currents were chilly, but warmer than in winter, so they didn't pull him so hard toward the ground. Only mild bumps rocked him gently along his way. The flarote bulb had healed his many wounds and he flew with the vigor of his youth, marveling at the sparkling sky above the pouring rains. He flew with such urgency that he reached Centaur River and the edge of the Black Forest shortly after the sun peeked over the distant clouds.

As he flew he thought of the woman, Anna, and Jarek and his wife. He didn't know if he could ever repay them in full for what they'd been willing to sacrifice to help him, but he knew he must try. Jarek obviously held his beliefs very close, but having to choose between two of them, he had done the most merciful thing Hiro could have believed of any human.

Boorda, too, in her way, had helped him. Not only by helping Anna, as was her duty according to her oaths, but not asking questions saved more lives than her own. When Hiro thought back to the moment he'd allowed a tear to leak from his eye at the torturous hands of Shampy, he knew in his heart that these two frail humans, Jarek and Boorda, were meeker than he could ever be. That made them stronger than himself and anyone else he knew. He couldn't allow any harm to come to these unique human specimens.

Once the sun burned bright at his side, Hiro decided to dip below the clouds for a rest. He saw a spot by Centaur River where he could sleep on the rocks, but under a large tree to minimize the rain. He wondered briefly if he might find the centaurs in the area again until he saw a large gray dragon crawl out from under the trees.

"Clear skies, Rakgar!" he hailed the leader as he landed on the rocks next to him. "What brings you out of the Rock Clouds?"

The mighty gray dragon jerked his head toward the trees. "I was too anxious for your return." He loped into the forest beside the river with Hiro close behind and curled up on damp grass under a tree. "I wanted to hear from you as soon as possible."

Hiro tucked his legs under him in front of Rakgar. "Didn't you get a report from Tog?" He had to figure out how much Tog had relayed before he could answer anything. Did the great troll collapse under pressure?

"Yes," Rakgar said, "but he couldn't give me many memories. He said Shampy told you how to destroy the creature and you saw it for yourselves, but on the way back you were attacked. He said he left you injured in the wilderness only at your insistence."

Before Hiro could open his mouth they heard trampling behind them. "There he is! I knew I saw him. I told you he would get here quickly! Hiro, you must have flown faster than even Tomgryn to get here so fast." Prakyndar's excited, nasal voice arrived ahead of him with Tog at his side. "Did you see the creature, Hiro? Did you fight it? Did it hurt you? Will you tell me all about it? I'd love to get a look at it! I passed the Krusible, Hiro! But of course you can see that, can't you? I can help you now. I'll always be at your call. You'll never have to leave me behind again! Can I go fight the creature with Hiro, Rakgar?"

Once he took a breath, Hiro nodded at the little dragon bouncing among the trees. "Congratulations on passing the Krusible, Prak. But I don't know if you're ready to deal with this creature." He turned back to Rakgar. "Did Tog tell you it's a wraith?"

Rakgar nodded, but Tog intervened. "I told him I left you in the wilderness when you were injured. I told him how you insisted I get this information back to him as soon as possible." He gave Hiro a knowing look and Hiro felt guilty for ever doubting his best friend.

"So your visit to Shampy was helpful?" Rakgar asked.

"Yes," Hiro said, "she gave us the means to destroy the wraith. I'm sure it would be a simple matter with less than ten dragons to aid."

Hiro was not surprised at the next sound. "I'll help, Hiro!" Prak practically screamed. "I'll do whatever you need me to do. I can't wait to see you in action! I bet you could handle that monster all by yourself! But I'll be there to back you up. I even fought a little with Milah at the Krusible. He tried to push me around, but I showed him he couldn't treat me like that. I'm faster than most might think! I could surround that beast all by myself! I would—"

Prak's exclamations of bravado died with Rakgar's single raised eyebrow. In the silence, Rakgar growled. "No one is going after this creature."

"But—" Hiro started.

"No," Rakgar said again. "A wraith is no concern of the dragons'. Let it kill off the human pestilence and do us a favor."

"But Rakgar," Hiro stammered, "don't you understand? If this wraith is allowed reign, it will kill off the humans along with our food supply. The humans don't even know what it is, nor how to deal with it."

"Do you plan to tell them?"

Hiro glanced at Tog. He remained silent, staring at the ground. "Of course not, Rakgar."

"Do you still have this ribbon Shampy gave you?"

Hiro looked into his claw as if it might appear. "I must have dropped it when I was injured," he concocted.

"Good," the leader nodded, "let it lay. If someone finds it and knows how to use it, fine. If not..." He couldn't finish the unpleasant thought.

Hiro could hear the plink of rain against their scales. He realized that even Prak knew the gravity of the situation enough to remain silent. Turning to the other two dragons, he said, "Could I speak with Rakgar alone for a few moments, please?"

Both dragons nodded and ran further into the forest. When they were well out of hearing, Hiro finally faced his leader. "I'm going back." Rakgar's face didn't twitch. "With the name 'Hiro' came a new respect for the rules and the reasons we follow them, but I've seen humans do things I never thought them capable of."

Finally, Rakgar's stone face moved only to lift an eyebrow again. "Oh? Like what?"

Hiro's mind searched only briefly. "A human woman actually protected her child. From what we're taught she should have thrown him to the wraith to allow her escape, but she actually placed herself between them."

"Humans will do odd things at times, I have no doubt." Rakgar tilted his head. "Or have you grown fond of the creatures?"

"Not overly," but Hiro dropped his gaze again. "You know I don't want to go against your word. Perhaps it's a childish whim, but I beg you not to forbid me from returning."

After a long silence, Rakgar growled and leveled his eyes at Hiro. "I won't forbid you, but I won't order any help for you." He sat up to his full height again, bringing him at least five claws taller than Hiro. "If you do this, you do it alone."

Hiro said nothing. He wouldn't ask anyone to go with him. It would be too dangerous, even if they never met Anna.

Rakgar stalked to the river bank. "I must return to the Rock Clouds. I'm sure you want to rest." When he reached the banks, with rainy skies above, he turned back to Hiro one last time. "Come home safely, Hiro Tekla. Shining days to you."

"Rakgar," Hiro stepped toward him, "I hoped to hear—that is, I wonder if—has Priya returned to the Rock Clouds while I was away?"

Rakgar narrowed his eyes and rumbled in the back of his throat. "No. She has not come home yet." He avoided Hiro's eyes as he mumbled, "We must pray to Tartaku that you will both return safely."

Hiro dipped his head, but he felt no hope in his leader's words. "Clear skies to you, Rakgar," he muttered back. The mighty gray dragon lifted into the sky with enormous wings beating the rain back. Once he was gone, Tog and Prak ran up behind him.

"Did Rakgar leave?" Prak asked, bounding forward. "Is he going back? He's not going to fight the creature himself, is he? I could imagine him thinking it was entirely his own responsibility. He's a good leader like that, isn't he? You must have made him see things your way, right, Hiro? I have a good mind to go find that thing myself, but I'll do whatever you want, Hiro. Just ask."

Hiro listened absently to Prak's prattle while eyeing Tog. When the little creature stopped, Hiro opened his mouth. "You have a mate now, Tog. Go back to her."

"Tog has a mate? Who is it? Is it Hesakin? Memador? Oh! Is it Supinga? Or—wait, why are you telling him to go back?" Prak's questions died with a glance from Hiro.

"I always knew you would do this." Tog bared his teeth in disgust. "From the moment—" he glanced at Prak, "from the moment the creature appeared, I knew you would do it."

"And your place is in the Rock Clouds with your mate."

Tog stepped closer to Hiro. He stretched out his neck to stare one eye directly into Hiro's face. "Just be careful. Not everything is worth dying for." Without another word, Tog ripped past the other two dragons and launched himself into the sky just short of the river bank. Hiro watched him soar toward the Rock Clouds before he turned to Prak.

"You can't come either, Prakyndar."

"That's what you think! I'll have you know, I'm a fully accepted member of the Rock Cloud Ruck now. I passed the Krusible. I took the Oath of Silence in front of Rakgar and most of the ruck. I'm allowed to go to the surface whenever I please now. Just like you! You can't make me go back. I don't have a mate to answer to. I'm going to help you whether you like it or not!" A final jerk of his head sent a ripple down the spikes along his back and he sat up straight as a tree trunk.

"Prak, this will be dangerous." Hiro curled up on the ground. He had been flying all night, he could use some rest.

"Don't worry, I'll be the best dragon to have by your side. You'll see! I'll do whatever you say. I'll—"

"Will you be quiet?" Hiro interrupted as his head lolled on top of his claws.

"Of course I will!" Prak said in a lower voice. "You'll see. You'll be happy I'm here! I'll let you sleep. You'll forget I'm even here. I'll keep watch for a while and then get some sleep myself. I'll need my rest, too, for our adventures together."

His voice droned off into quiet mumbles about the many exciting things they would do together and as Hiro's mind filled with sleep, another thought came to him. But before he could voice it, he drifted off.

———

"The centaurs!" Hiro sat up, wide awake.

Beside him, Prak snorted out of a dead sleep and rolled over. "What about them?"

"I have to go see them."

"Really?" Prak bounced to his claws. "I've never met a centaur before! I hear they're friendly. And tall. Taller than me! Do you know many centaurs? Of course you do, you met them before, didn't you?"

Hiro tried not to go into detail about his doings while on the surface the first time. Rakgar told him it would send a bad message to younger dragons that erroneous deeds might go unpunished, so he refrained. But Prak, with his needling, had gotten at least a little more information than others who had tried.

"Yes," he answered the younger dragon, "I've met the Leader of the Warrior Centaurs. Her name is Ashel."

"Wow! I can't wait to meet her! I bet she could even put Milah and Mitashio in their place. At the same time! I—" When his voice stopped suddenly, Hiro twisted his neck to inspect the younger dragon. Prak scratched sharp claws at his belly. "Should we hunt first? I haven't eaten for a while. I would hate to be rude while we're with the centaurs."

"Perhaps we should hunt along the way," Hiro nodded. "The centaur land is very far from here. And it's been quite a while since I fed, as well."

He stepped toward the river bank in order to gain the dripping sky, but Prak ran up beside him. "But, Hiro, didn't Rakgar tell you? He said some centaurs passed through here not too long ago. I wasn't around to meet them and he said they left quickly. That was just before you arrived. They headed north. They shouldn't be more than a day ahead of us!"

The smile on Prak's face reminded Hiro of the panting dogs in Jarek's barn. He remembered that Prak only wished to please. "Very good, we probably won't have to hunt along the way, then."

Prak's maw snapped shut. "Why not?"

"It's centaur etiquette to feed their guests."

"Really?" Prak almost bounced on the spot. "We get to eat with the centaurs, too?"

"I don't think we should rely on it, though." Hiro spread his wings and pressed himself into the downpour, calling back to Prak, "What I have to ask them probably won't make us guests for long."

27

EXPECTATIONS

The two dragons dropped amidst a torrential storm. They had flown for some time above the clouds, but decided late in the day to search under the clouds. Hiro put his sensitive smell to work and found a trace of the centaurs sharp enough to follow. Luckily enough, with Hiro's sharp day vision, he soon spotted a black centaur waving to him in the forest beneath them.

Of course, he thought to himself, *if the creature hadn't moved I never would've seen him under the trees.*

Prak burbled on about Hiro's keen vision, day and night, while the two lowered themselves carefully through the trees. Once they landed, Hiro recognized the black centaur as the one that had saved Surneen's life in her memory.

"You!" he said without thinking. The centaur's entire body was almost as black as Hiro's. He wore the bracers and cannon-bone armor of a warrior. But the sword on his back and the knives on his hips didn't intimidate Hiro more than the scar he had failed to notice in Surneen's memory. The pinched scar ran down his cheek and jaw, skipped his neck and followed through to his shoulder and arm. Where it met his cheek, his lips pulled down in a permanent frown, but Hiro wondered if the warrior always wore a stern look, anyway.

The centaur paused only a moment before touching his fingers to the bridge of his nose. "Have we met, dragon?" His voice was deep and firm, but Hiro could hear the centaur friendliness in it.

Hiro shook his head, and responded by respectfully touching his claws first to his forehead, then to his nose-bridge and then to his chest. Dipping his head last, he said, "You saved the life of my best friend's mate, Surneen. She's a red and orange dragon. Her hunting group was attacked by humans some sun cycles ago."

"Ah, yes," he nodded, but his lips thinned in anger at the memory, "the trap. We've been searching out such traps and destroying them ever since." He placed a hand on his bare chest. "My name is Vikal."

"I'm called Hiro." He knew better than to invoke his full Faerie-tongue-based name with the centaurs. They would only consider it a vulgarity. Hiro dipped his head and nodded to Prak. "This is Prak. The sharpest dragon I know."

Prak dipped his head. "Well met, Vikal. I've never met a centaur before. By The One! You really are taller than me! I bet you could pin me to the ground under one hoof! But you wouldn't have to by the looks of that sword. That must be as long as my leg!"

Vikal grinned at the compliment. "Well met, Prak. How can I serve two mighty dragons?"

"I wonder," Hiro began tentatively, "if you travel with Ashel?"

Vikal nodded. "We travel with Ashel and Joss, himself. I am second to Ashel and go where she goes."

"I need to speak to both of them, if it's possible?"

"Of course." Vikal placed two fingers in front of his lips. He looked past Hiro into the trees beyond and blew three short whistles.

When Hiro peered through the trees, a dappled gray centaur seemed to appear through the sheet of rain. Vikal waved his arms this way and that in what must have been some sort of signal. The other centaur responded in kind with only small differences. Vikal trotted further north as the gray centaur dissolved back into the rain.

"Come," he waved his arm at the dragons. "Any friend of Ashel's."

As they sloshed through the rain and trees, Prak asked all kinds of questions of Vikal, giving Hiro time to think of what he would say to Joss and Ashel. The centaur told them their group had once tracked humans through this area and scattered them when dragons weren't around for the humans to prey on. Only in the occurrence with Surneen's group had they been forced to engage the humans. Just as Vikal recounted to Prak how many humans he had killed, they caught sight of several leafy canopies tucked into the trees.

The largest had three fires burning in front of it. As they approached, Hiro saw three lydik roasting over the fires with tree branches stretched overhead for protection from the rain.

"You came just in time," Vikal gestured toward the cooking fires. "We were afraid we might have to dry and carry all this meat ourselves. Now we can share it with you. That should please Joss."

Just as Prak started to ask why the centaurs referred to their leader by his own name, Hiro saw Ashel step out of the large canopy. With a grin of recognition, she moved out of the way to let two more centaurs follow her.

Ashel was a dark brown centaur with matching hair that flowed down her back into her mane. The two centaurs behind her must have been her brothers because they were the same color with bronze skin as well. There were two striking differences between the males. One wore a leather band wrapped around his head along with a stole of black-and-white striped fur over one shoulder. The other wore no fur but had a brilliant silver sword strapped to his back. They both wore the bracers and cannon-bone armor of the warriors.

"Dak!" Ashel called to him. She touched the bridge of her nose as the shortened warrior greeting. "In trouble again already?"

She and her brothers skirted the cooking fires to meet them. Hiro touched his forehead, nose bridge and chest three times, to greet each of them. "Actually, I'm called Hiro now," he answered her.

"Hiro? Your first visit must have been a great success." She glanced to Hiro's side with a crooked smile. "And who is your friend?"

Hiro glanced twice at Prak, who stood rooted on the spot with his maw hanging open. "This is Prak. He's never met centaurs before."

Before Hiro could apologize for Prak's gauche, the little dragon stumbled forward and poked himself in the eye a couple of times before accomplishing the centaur greeting. "I'm truly honored to meet you." He dipped his head so low his nose almost stuck in the mud. When he raised it again, his jaws had still not closed. When Ashel's smile widened, he added, "You are the fiercest and most beautiful creature I've ever seen in my life."

"Careful, Prak," Hiro grinned at him, "your heart might break for a centaur."

With wide eyes only for Ashel, he answered, "Would that be so bad?"

Ashel turned her smile to Hiro, but jerked her head at Prak. "Well, this one can stay."

Hiro left the swooning to Prak while he approached the others. The male with the shining sword only touched his forehead in greeting. "I'm Rylan. I believe we saw each other when you met Ashel before. I'm sorry we didn't get a chance to speak then."

The other male with the leather band and fur touched his forehead, nose bridge and chest. "Well met, Hiro. I'm Joss, Ruler of the Centaurs. And Ashel's brother." He added the last for Prak's benefit.

"Brother?" Prak bounced in front of Hiro to fumble his way through the centaur greeting again. "Wow,

I get to meet a beautiful centaur and the centaur ruler all in one day! This is the best first trip to the surface I could've imagined." He cocked his head back to Hiro but didn't quite contain his whisper. "Lifkar will never believe this!"

Joss motioned toward the fires with a grin. "I'm afraid we can't accommodate you both in our little shelters, but we will still be pleased to have your company."

Other centaurs came and left while they ate. Hiro supposed they were rotating duties as lookouts. Vikal, Ashel, Rylan and Joss all folded their legs under them to sit on the ground. Hiro and Prak did the same.

Hiro allowed Prak's natural flow of questions to take over the conversation. Prak asked about the centaur greeting, the centaurs' love of the stars, their hierarchy and culture and much more. He mostly gazed at Ashel, who tried her best to answer his questions, but he listened intently to all of the centaurs in their turn.

The group talked and ate until the sun went down. The centaurs ate an entire lydik amongst themselves and Prak and Hiro shared another. With his stomach well full of fire, Prak offered to quickly dry out the meat on the remaining lydik so the centaurs wouldn't have to linger for days waiting for it to dry. Hiro only helped him a little.

Well into the night, Prak finally brought the conversation to their most current adventure. "Hiro sat straight up, out of a dead sleep," he told Ashel. "I was only drowsing because I was on guard duty, you know. But he insisted we must come visit the centaurs immediately before we could deal with the wraith."

"Wraith?!" Ashel waved away the rest of Prak's comments, looking sternly at Hiro. "What is this about?"

Hiro steeled himself against whatever reaction he might encounter. "You've heard about the creature attacking the humans, I suppose?"

"We've heard rumors," Joss glanced at Rylan, but continued to Hiro, "but it hasn't bothered the centaurs. Is it really a wraith?"

Hiro nodded. "According to a faerie shaman named Shampy."

"What did this faerie demand as payment?" Joss asked.

"Blood and a tear, but she ended up with marrow, also." Hiro remembered the excruciation all too well.

"Marrow?" Joss's mouth twisted in disgust. "That's a heavy price to ask, even for a faerie. What did she give you in return? Something more than just misinformation, I hope."

"She told us what kind of creature had been conjured, where it was and how to kill it." Hiro rolled his shoulder again at the thought of not having the ribbon with him. "She also gave us a ribbon that could be used to kill it, but I lost it."

"It's just as well you did." Rylan hadn't spoken for most of the evening, but his voice was a strong, loud tenor now. "If any human majishun caught you with it, they might have killed you. Or at least died trying."

"Why? What was it?" Hiro could sense Rylan knew more than he was saying. When Joss motioned for his brother to speak, even Prak sat quiet with anticipation.

"The ribbon," Rylan swallowed the word as if he swallowing a week-old liver, "is made of human skin, carefully peeled, slowly, in one continual strip, with majikal means while the unfortunate victim is still alive."

Hiro's top lip bared his fangs in horror and a little anger. Prak made a gurgle in his throat.

Ashel shook her head. "Tartaku curse them."

Hiro knew the centaurs held no love for humans, but they wouldn't torture any creature, even the ones they hunted. Death to others, when necessary, was always as quick and as painless as they could make it. Although their zeal brought death more often than not upon creatures who crossed them, they tried to avoid inflicting pain on anyone. Except, maybe, faeries.

"A wraith conjured from the dirt," Rylan continued, "is afraid of two things. Human skin and dragon fire. Those two things together will kill an Earth Wraith, sending it back to the dirt."

"Rylan," Joss interjected, "is not only a fierce warrior, but he is also brave enough to dabble in majik. It's most useful when dealing with faeries. He knows all the centaur majishuns and majikal happenings and I'm glad he fights for us."

Many of the centaurs touched their foreheads to Rylan, who ignored their gestures. Hiro scratched absently at the ground under his claw, carefully watching while Rylan took a long pull from a water skin. Finally Hiro rolled his shoulder again. "Then it would be Rylan to whom I should put my next question."

The shining silver sword on his back seemed to glow and call for Hiro's neck while Rylan wiped his mouth with the back of his hand. "Speak it, dragon."

"Shampy said the centaurs conjured the wraith."

Chaos erupted around them. Several centaurs, many on their feet, unsheathed swords and knocked arrows onto bows. Everyone shouted at once. Prak jumped to his feet, denying any knowledge and arguing for the centaurs. Ashel had knives in her hand before Prak was on his feet. She accused him of sneaking into their camp with false friendship. Vikal yelled for them to leave. Even Joss roared about the faeries' accusations. All the while, Rylan and Hiro never twitched, their eyes in a dead lock.

Finally, Joss lifted his hands. "Peace!" he yelled over the tumult. The group fell silent, but not a single weapon resumed its sheath.

Joss stared at Rylan, but Rylan's eyes kept Hiro's. Slowly, Rylan took a small step forward. Hiro didn't move. He sat casually with his legs in front of him. Rylan took another step forward. Hiro didn't move. Rylan took two steps forward. Hiro pushed his head forward ever so slightly to prove that Rylan couldn't intimidate him.

Eventually, in the silence, Rylan turned to meet Joss's stare. "He is not our enemy."

As Ashel tucked her knives away, a few more centaurs did the same. Hiro faced Joss calmly. "I came to you for the truth. If I wanted more lies I would've gone to another faerie."

At these words the rest of the company put away their weapons. With sighs and grumbles of complaints about the evening's interruption they either plodded away or rested again. Rylan stepped back to Joss's side.

"But," Joss spread his hands, "it doesn't matter what we say. It will always be our word against theirs."

Before Hiro could tell him how much more the centaurs' word meant to him over the faeries', Rylan spoke again. "That is the most damning evidence against your faerie, of course. She probably hoped it would come down to our word against hers, but you can discover the truth yourself."

"What do you mean?" Hiro asked, but he could see the same question in Joss's and Ashel's eyes.

"Have you seen the wraith yet?"

"Yes," Hiro settled back on his haunches, "in Eoaa on this side of the Torthoth Mountains."

Rylan folded his arms across his broad chest. "When you asked this faerie about who conjured the wraith, she simply said the centaurs had, correct?"

Hiro nodded. "I asked her if Joss was aware of the conjuring, but she didn't know the name or who he was. I haven't trusted much of what she said either before that or since."

"Wise," Ashel added, still fingering a knife hilt.

"When you saw the wraith," Rylan asked, "did it travel with a long trail of shadow behind it? Was it forced to retrace the path of the shadow?"

Hiro thought back to his encounter. When the wraith came through the window after Anna, it did not flee around the outside of the house as he would have expected. "Yes," he whispered, "it did."

"Then you can still discover the true conjurer." Hiro's eyes again met Rylan's, but by this time he wore a smug grin. "You see, it takes a powerful majishun to conjure a wraith. Once done, that majishun is bound to the wraith. He sees what the wraith sees. Some say he experiences what the wraith experiences. No one really knows unless they've done it, and many simply die from the experience. What we do know from observation is that if the wraith is too powerful for the majishun, the majishun can break the bond. Of course, then you have a powerful and dangerous monster on the loose. But if the majishun is powerful enough or motivated enough, they can keep the connection and somewhat control the monster."

"Control it?" Joss's voice sounded even more appalled at that idea.

"Yes," Rylan's eyes never came from Hiro. "It's difficult—"

"—it did seem as if the wraith struggled against an unseen force—" Hiro put in.

"—but it's possible for the majishun to force it to only attack who he wants it to attack. Make it go where he wants it to go—"

"—and make it seem as if someone else is the enemy."

"If you follow the trail of shadow to its source, you'll know exactly who conjured the wraith. Hiro," Rylan waited until Hiro met his eyes again, "I have my own crystal ball. The wraith will be on the other side of the pass from Kingstor Noble in three days' time."

Lost in his own thoughts, Hiro didn't notice the silence except for the rain around him. Finally, he twisted his neck back around to face Prak. "I know what I need you to do."

28

RULES

Much to Prak's disappointment, the two dragons slept outside the centaur camp the night after their discussion with Rylan. After accusations like his, Hiro wasn't surprised when they were asked to leave. They spent the next two days flying over the Black Forest and the Torthoth Mountains, well above the cloud line. Hiro remembered very well the many humans on the mountains standing in their way.

"Why are we flying over the clouds again?" Prak asked Hiro as they flew away from the sun. "I can't see where we're going!"

"Can't you sense direction?"

"I can sense direction, but I've never been this far—well, I've never been anywhere but the Rock Clouds, have I? How can I possibly sense where we are in the landscape, if I've never been there and don't even know what it looks like? I mean, I know there's a mountain range. I've seen one or two of your memories—small memories, passed around the ruck—but I've never been there for myself. If it wasn't for this cursed rain we could fly under the clouds and I could see the entire land!"

"We're over the mountains now," he told the smaller dragon. "If you want to fly under the clouds I'm sure there will be plenty of humans willing to shoot you down."

"I know you told me the humans have watches set up in the mountains, but why are we flying so far south? I mean, I—"

"We're not flying 'so far south,'" he yelled to the younger dragon. "This is where you need to go." With a great effort he pulled himself steady in the air. Prak did the same. Pumping his wings, Hiro pointed with his front claw. "You need to fly north over the mountains. There. You know what to do."

Prak dipped his head twice. "You can count on me. I know what to do. I'll be back before you know it. I told you I'll do whatever you want me to do. I—"

"Prak!" Hiro called as the brown dragon started to fly away. Prak turned and hovered a moment longer in question. "I am glad you're here."

"Ha!" Prak's snort sounded halfway between laugh and a roar. "I told you you'd be happy!" He spun away to the north where Hiro ordered him. "I'm always good to have around. Now maybe everyone will believe me when I tell them I can help. I'm not just a pretty hide. I'm useful. I work hard. I won't let you down! I'm—"

Hiro didn't hear anything else Prak said. His voice dropped along with his wings into the clouds. Hiro silently hoped the little dragon's constant chatter wouldn't get him into trouble.

As for the rest of his plan, he hadn't shared it with Prak. Prak knew Hiro was going to try to take on the wraith. Hiro had said he might try to find the ribbon, but he didn't mention that humans needed to be involved. Hiro flew further south. Once the sun had truly set, he sank through the clouds.

——

He took the long way around. Very long. The wraith would reach Jarek and the Hamees' village the very next night, but Hiro couldn't come at them from the north. Every path from the north crawled with humans. Hiro prayed silently to Tartaku that Prak had already finished what he needed to do and was headed safely back to the Black Forest.

Hiro landed and crept across the muddy expanse of fields. He left tracks along the small ribbon of water, between some trees, through a few fields and probably even too close to some of the houses. He avoided animal pens as much as he could because he knew the excited critters would awaken their owners. His tracks would cause enough commotion when the sun rose unless Hiro could get to Jarek before their discovery.

As he side-stalked a shelter full of feathery birds, he paused for the thousandth time debating on what to do next. It might be possible to win Jarek's assistance without speaking to him. No. He shook himself and kept crawling. He would have to explain to the human what was coming and the importance of getting the ribbon from Anna. It might take Jarek most of the day, as it had last time, to get to Kingstor and back. Hiro couldn't wait for Jarek to figure out what needed to be done without addressing him directly.

Hiro rolled his shoulder when Jarek's barn came into view. The rain fell in a fine trickle, allowing him to see the human structures properly.

The sun must be up, he growled to himself. *I've wasted enough time. Let's get this over with.*

He crossed through the open space behind Jarek's home, leaving a blatant trail for the man to find him. Behind the barn he curled his tail around him and lay on his belly. Now he waited.

The dogs in the barn stirred and gave small yips as they recognized the scent of the dragon. But not enough to call attention to him. Only a moment later the hatch on the home creaked open. Hiro could hear someone shuffling out of the house onto the sodden ground. As the footsteps stopped outside the barn, Hiro realized that the sound of the stride seemed wrong.

The dogs inside the barn barked once, then twice. He could hear them panting and frolicking. The human footsteps paused at the door of the barn. Hiro watched the edge of the barn until Boorda stepped into view.

She threw a hand to her throat and sucked enough air into her lungs to wake the five kingdoms at once if she loosed it. But she didn't scream. With eyes the size of a centaur's, the human stared at the black dragon. Both creatures froze.

Hiro had only planned on confronting Jarek, not his mate. He briefly debated inquiring after Jarek, but dismissed the idea. He couldn't go that far.

As he pondered what could be done, Boorda's hand slid down to her stomach. She swallowed. "You!" She scrutinized Hiro, but kept her hand at her waist, clutching her dress. "You're her dragon, aren't you?"

How in the frozen waste did she know that?

"Look at me," Boorda said to herself, "talking like you understand me."

The human squished her face together as if she was in pain. Squinting through one eye, she reached out one hand—toward Hiro's nose.

If pet I must be…, Hiro thought.

With a silent sigh, he allowed the woman's hand to touch his nose. Her face smoothed and she even smiled a little as she ran her fingers up the dragon's snout and around his eyes. Her hand was soft. As soft as Anna's. Her face was gentle and kind. Much more than Anna's, if not as beautiful. When she scratched hard behind the spine flap covering his ear, Hiro couldn't help but roll his eyes and enjoy it.

"You're just a big cuddle bear, aren't you?" Boorda asked with a grin, but Hiro didn't care about the remark. It did feel good. She stroked his head one last time then put her hands on her hips. "Jarek thinks I'm so frail as to be protected from you." Shaking her head, she added, "You probably feel the same way about that princess of yours." Hiro tilted his head to the side. "But you mark my word," she briefly stared past him into the distance, "there's dragon in that woman. More than I've ever seen before."

Hiro clenched his jaw to stop himself from questioning her statement. "You must be looking for her," Boorda squinted at him. "She's not here." She raised her voice as if speaking to a hatchling. "Anna's not here." She shook her head and threw up her hands. "There, I've gone and said her name. Now you'll think she's coming." She held out both hands to him firmly with palms toward him. "Stay here. Stay." She gathered her rain-soaked skirts and stepped back around the corner of the barn.

Mustn't seem too complacent, Hiro thought, but he only stretched his neck to follow the woman around the corner.

"Eh, eh!" she snapped, wheeling on him and smacking his nose. "I said 'stay'!" She pointed behind him and only out of pure shock at such treatment did he settle back into his waiting place—maybe a little too quickly.

He listened as she marched back into the home. "Jarek," she called none-too-quietly, "there's someone here you need to see."

Other footsteps clomped through the house. That tread was more familiar. "Who's that?"

"Behind the barn." Hiro could imagine Boorda's mischievous grin at her mate. After more shuffling and a sigh, Boorda added, "Be careful with that one." Jarek's movement ceased. "Seems he'll need a firm hand." With that Hiro knew he could hear the smile on her face.

"Boorda, I—" Jarek started to stammer, but his wife cut him short.

"Just go, you hairy lydik. Your 'someday' is come."

I'll never make sense of these humans, Hiro thought to himself as Jarek tromped through the muddy yard to reach him.

When the human man turned the corner, his face wore no surprise at seeing a large black dragon waiting for him. "She's not here," he said, shaking his head.

Hiro set himself firmly. Was he really going to do this?

"I told you, she's not here." Jarek waved his arms in front of him. "You must go."

Now that he was face-to-face with the man, Hiro couldn't decide what to say first. *I'm here for you*? Or maybe *I know she's not here*?

"Anna's at the castle." Jarek threw both hands in the direction of Kingstor. "The castle!"

Hiro's nerves boiled in his belly. He should tell the man of the danger coming.

Jarek sighed, dropping his hands to his sides. "Perhaps it's better that you're here."

Hiro cocked his head. *Maybe I'll just listen for a moment. Something might come to me.*

"There's rumor of you coming this way." Jarek leaned against the barn wall. "They say you've been killing hundreds of people along the way." He squinted at the dragon. "I don't suppose you could explain that, could you?" Hiro laid his head on the ground. "No, of course not." Jarek shook his head. "I can't imagine you killing for no reason. Certainly not if Anna didn't want it."

Now he was reaching the right conclusions. This man really was smarter than the rest.

"There must be something out there." Jarek stared toward the mountains. "Something killing humans. Something dangerous is coming."

'I'll help you,' Hiro thought of saying, but he only lifted his head from the ground.

Jarek reached his hand out like he was petting a faithful old dog. Stroking Hiro's snout, he said, "We could probably use you if it comes here. You and your fire."

When he said the last word Hiro allowed a burst of flame to tickle his lips well away from the man's hand. Jarek yanked his hand away nonetheless.

Staring hard at the dragon, Jarek stood up. "Commands," he said, nodding, "Anna must use commands."

Simple, but hopefully effective, Hiro thought.

Jarek looked around. He picked up one of his tools from behind the barn. Holding the metal end with the handle pointed away from him, he pointed at the wood end facing Hiro. "Fire!" he said firmly.

Hiro almost smiled. He belched just enough hot flame onto the wooden handle to light it despite the water.

As Jarek watched it burn, he yelled with joy. He threw the ruined tool into the soggy ground and looking back at the dragon, he said, "At least now we have a weapon."

But they needed more. Anna must still have the ribbon. *'It won't help,'* Hiro knew he must tell the man. *'We need something more.'*

"I'll gather the other men in the village," Jarek stared at the ground while he planned.

'It won't be enough to kill the creature,' Hiro knew he must tell him. *'Go to Kingstor and get the ribbon from Anna.'*

"I'll have to tell them about you, but considering what you did for us before and what you might do for us now, I don't think anyone, even Gullin, could take issue. And who would dare, anyway?"

Hiro thought, *I'll start with just his name. The rest will come later.* His stomach churned as he opened his mouth.

29

IMPRESSING

"Jarek!" Hiro's jaw snapped shut when he heard the call. Jarek spun around the corner of the barn to follow the voice. Hiro did the same with his head.

"Anna!" Jarek answered her.

She strode tall and straight toward them. "I thought I would find you both here." She joined them behind the barn. "Hiro's claw prints are being noticed in the village. Apparently he hasn't been as careful as he usually is."

Jarek held up both hands to her. "It's alright. I was going to gather the others, anyway."

"Good," she nodded. "We'll need all the help we can get. My brother refuses to listen to reason. We're on our own. Do you know what's coming?"

"No," he answered. For the first time, concern creased his brow. "Is it that bad?"

"Worse." She stared at Hiro a moment before turning back to Jarek. "Gather the men. I'll explain everything and Hiro and I will help you save your village."

Jarek nodded. "We'll meet you in front of the sanctuary." He turned to leave, but stopped. "Oh, and I think I figured out one of the commands you use. For 'Fire!', anyway."

When he said the word for Anna's benefit, Hiro barely remembered that he was supposed to respond. But he recovered and snorted a quick flame from his nostrils, enough for Jarek to point out his success.

Anna grinned at the exchange. "Yes, well, Hiro and I have plenty of surprises."

Once Jarek was well out of hearing, Anna turned her sharp eyes on the dragon. "Did you...?"

"No." But he didn't admit that she'd interrupted them just in time. "You couldn't get any soldiers?"

She shook her head. "I believe Philip would help if he understood everything, but by that time it would be far too late."

Hiro rolled his shoulder. "Remember," he told her, "tell the men to draw it in by boiling salt water, but the fire must be made with men's fire, not dragon fire."

"I know, Hiro."

"The—ribbon," he hesitated even mentioning the disgusting item. "Do you still have it?"

She reached into a hidden pocket of her riding dress. "Yes," she said, holding it up for him to see.

"Then I'll wait here." He jerked his head to point behind her. "Go gather your soldiers."

———

When a hatchling is introduced to the ruck, many friends of the sires will visit the lair and see the young one. Hiro felt this sharp sense of display sitting behind the barn. Men came in small groups to see the dragon. Jarek once pulled the burnt handle of the tool out of the mud and made Hiro burn it again for the others.

At one point Hiro caught sight of little Harry far off in a field. The little boy stared at him in wonder until his mother ran out and scooped him up. She didn't even glance in the dragon's direction, but her avoidance somehow screamed louder than the men staring.

After Jarek finished showing them Hiro's ability to help, the men stacked great loads of wood on sledges and covered them with oilcloth to keep them dry. A strange black cauldron with a concave bottom, large enough to boil Hiro's head, was loaded behind Jarek's horse. Piles upon piles of long, metal-tined implements were stacked next to everything.

Before Hiro could imagine, the sky began to darken. He couldn't tell if the sun had set or if the darkness came from the clouds thickening. The rain intensified as the men gathered in front of Hiro. Most of them tried not to stare, but none of them could keep their eyes from him for very long.

More horses were brought to pull the other sledges. The skittish beasts were quickly contained by their owners. Rika's own horse pulled the heavy cauldron.

Finally, Anna and Jarek stepped out of Jarek's home. "I'm not trying to make a political statement," Jarek said quietly, "but the Hamees feel it is the man's duty to protect women." He scurried next to her and Hiro noticed she had changed her dress for a baggy pair of men's pants, shirt and a vest.

"And my brother would probably agree with you," she answered while pulling on a pair of leather gloves. "But seeing as he's not here and I'm still your sovereign princess, I'll be going with you and my dragon."

"Anna, you should stay with the women. They could use your strength." Jarek abandoned his own principles, grabbing her arm and spinning her to face him.

Without thinking Hiro snorted, shooting a glob of fire in front of Jarek's foot. The man eyed Hiro as if waiting for an attack.

Stupid human, Hiro thought, *doesn't he realize that females are probably better equipped to handle such situations?*

Anna erased the surprise on her face at Hiro's actions. She gently removed Jarek's hand from her arm. "Hiro will need my guidance more. If we're going to be successful, I'll need to be there to help."

"You've told us all you know, I'm sure we can—"

"Jarek, we've been over this," she looked him in the eye, but it came as more of a glare. "I'm coming with you." While he floundered for another argument, she took the opportunity to stride to Hiro. "I'll lead Hiro to the trees," she announced to the men. "Get the cauldron fire started."

Hiro lifted her onto his back without question. She leaned against him as he cantered into the fields. The men picked up their tools and began their long trudge into the fields.

Anna pointed out the same copse of trees Hiro had watched the village from some months ago. He thought how glad he was that he hadn't killed Jarek then.

"The men will light the fire under the cauldron inside their circle and set a ring of firewood around them," Anna said while he settled himself amongst the trees. "You can light the ring, can't you?" He glared at her. "Of course you can. I'll call for you when the wraith enters the ring. From there the matter will just be to tangle the thing with the ribbon." She watched momentarily as the men unloaded firewood further toward the mountains. "I wish I could figure out what it's made of!"

He paused, not knowing how much he should tell her. "I don't think—"

"You're right," she interrupted, "it's not important." She sighed. "Thank you for coming back."

"I'll do what I can," he told her. The rain picked up as she turned into it to run back to the Hamees men.

30

EVIL ENKINDLED

The black-shrouded shape moved head-first into the open space of the fields. Hiro couldn't see anything. The rain poured down in blankets. Hiro discovered the reasoning behind the concave-bottomed cauldron. The rainwater dripped over the sides, but the bell shape kept it from dousing the fire beneath. The water in the cauldron bubbled so much that it made the surface white, even in the pouring rain.

Hiro heard one of the men call out and thought it sounded like Rika. As they waited for the monster to inch closer to them, they unwittingly tightened the circle they'd made with their bodies. The circle closed in toward the cauldron fire until only the heat kept them away.

"Surround it!" That command was definitely Rika's. His role as leader of their small village made him the natural leader of most enterprises. "Confuse it!"

The circle broke apart closest to the mountains, opening slowly and shifting to one side. Hiro clung to a thick oak trunk, trying to see as well as he could. He pried his claws out of the woody perch every so often. Finally, he heard what he'd been waiting for.

"HIRO!!!" Anna's scream could be heard for fells in every direction. He wouldn't have been surprised if her brother heard it within Kingstor Noble.

Hiro tumbled from the trees, snapping branches from his path. He burst from the copse in a hailstorm of twigs and leaves. Beating his wings, he roared as he flew straight toward the creature.

"FIRE!" Anna screamed, pointing to the stacks of wood surrounding the humans. Once he met the circle, Hiro bent his head over the firewood. Flying close to the stacks he pushed searing flame onto the wood. All around the men, the wood exploded in flame just as the straw in Jarek's barn. But rather than being frightened, the humans cheered at the sight of him.

Sweeping around the circle, Hiro noticed the thin trail of black coming from the wraith. Glancing in the direction of the mountains, he could see the tether to its creator creeping into blackness. However, the fire it crossed did nothing to harm the connection.

Most dragons can't hover long and Hiro was no exception. He swept around the blazing ring while the men within it fought the monster. Jarek held what Hiro had learned was a pitchfork, stabbing wildly at the wraith. Some men wielded axes; others, two short sticks with different shapes of spiked ends called dricklers.

The wraith, although mostly motionless, seemed more confused at the number of temptations than the manner in which they presented themselves. It shifted one way, then another. It would hold still and sway its head back and forth, then press toward another assailant.

Finally, the creature decided. One of the largest men, called Ammik, stood only inches taller than the others, but his broad shoulders and ample waist presented the tastiest morsel.

Ammik swung a heavy axe in each hand with ease. When he realized the wraith singled him out, he heaved them twice as fast. Faster and faster in a flowing pattern, the axes would have terrified a human, but they passed through the wraith as if made of smoke.

Ammik's axes dropped to the ground with two heavy thuds after they passed through the wraith, but he gathered his wits enough to pick them up and throw them out of the fire ring. Hiro was impressed with the courage the man showed when faced with such a monster. As the creature reached its black hands to take hold of Ammik on either side of his head, Hiro's fire roared between the two. Recoiling, the wraith wasn't exactly hurt, but it retreated from the man.

"Fire!" Rika yelled. "Use Hiro's fire to keep it away! The tools won't help, get them out of the way!"

The men threw their weapons out of the ring. The rain had soaked them too thoroughly to light without the dragon's help. Some of them landed in the fire, but with the rain beating down, they probably wouldn't light at all. Each of the twenty or so men picked up a log that Hiro had lit with his fire.

"Milo! Anna!" Rika yelled over the pounding rain. "The ribbon!" Anna threw one end of the ribbon to the man that must have been Milo. "Move it into the middle!" Rika ordered the men.

With their logs blazing before them, the men herded the monster into the middle of the ring, next to the boiling cauldron. Occasionally it attempted to grab a man with its black fingers, but they were easily evaded with a swipe of a burning log.

"Hiro!" Rika yelled as the men worked. "Fire!" he yelled, pointing to a break in the ring.

Hiro swept toward it and lit the saturated wood, but his effort was barely enough. The rain poured so hard that as soon as he re-lit one spot another would sputter out.

"Quickly!" Rika yelled to Anna and Milo. "Get it now! Now! NOW!"

Anna and Milo ran toward it. The other men ducked. The cord caught the creature in the middle, but didn't pass through like the tools. The pair ran toward each other, but the creature understood what was happening now. It grabbed one side of the ribbon and pulled the holder toward it.

Milo let go of the ribbon before the wraith could sweep him into its grasp. Another man jumped in front of him with the dragon fire to keep the wraith away from him. Milo scrabbled to get the end of the ribbon. Once he held it, he and Anna nodded and tried again.

Over and over, they tried to tangle the creature, but it continued to slip away. Rika tried distracting it. It sank down and spun away from the ribbon. Five men tried corralling it, but when one of their logs' flames went out, it slipped past them once more.

The men began to weary. They slipped in the mud. Their chests heaved from exertion. Faces creased with fear and worry.

Finally, Rika rallied them again. "More men!" he yelled while dropping his own log of dragon fire. "We need more men on the ribbon!" He held the ribbon in the middle with both hands. Three more men dropped their fires, which were dwindling in the deluge, to join him. "Ready?" Rika yelled. "Now!"

With the confusion of numerous attackers, the wraith didn't know where to look first. Rika ran straight into its face, wrapping the ribbon around its head. The wraith screamed and writhed on the spot. "Burn it!" he yelled over the monster's ear-piercing wail.

But the wraith was a caged animal now. And more dangerous than ever before. It managed to grab the two men on either side of Rika and swing them in a circle, knocking away the other men with their dragon fires in hand. Anna alone kept a tight hold of the ribbon, but got pulled to the ground for her effort.

Thrashing in Rika's grip, the wraith managed to ensnare itself. But when it lifted Rika into the air, he grabbed at the monster's head. Screaming more, the wraith and Rika fell to the ground in a jumble, yanking the ribbon from Anna's hand at last.

Rika and the wraith rolled on the ground together until they stopped next to the boiling cauldron. Rika scrambled away in the confusion on his belly and turned back to see the human flame under the cauldron catch the precious ribbon. The wraith remained unharmed and drifted smoothly upright while the last remains of the once-formidable ribbon floated harmlessly to the ground as ash.

31

SACRIFICE

"What do we do now?" Jarek yelled across to Anna.

"I don't know," she yelled back. She stared at her empty hands as she knelt on the ground. "I don't know what it was or how it was made." Her voice shook with maudlin tears. "I just don't know."

"We can't give up now!" Rika yelled, struggling to his feet. "It will move on to the village if we don't stop it!"

"But how?" Jarek searched the group for clues. In the meantime, Hiro continued sweeping around several open areas. "Hiro," he muttered.

But even Hiro had no idea what to do. He barely kept the creature contained. A dozen men held it at bay with logs barely on fire. The deluge of rain put out most of the fires.

Anna stumbled up beside Jarek. "Hiro is working hard enough to keep it contained. I don't think he can do anything more to help us."

Rika ran to Jarek. "Get the men out of here and back to safety," he told both Jarek and Anna. "I'll help Hiro keep it contained."

Anna shook her head. "It will follow us eventually."

"If only we had more dragons, perhaps—" Jarek started, but was cut off by a terrible roar nearby.

At first, Hiro thought it was just thunder then he wondered if Prak might be coming. Finally he bellowed his own roar to answer his best friend.

"Where did it come from?" Ammik called in amazement when Tog came into view.

"The Rock Clouds, I suppose!" Anna smiled.

"Is it like Hiro?" another man yelled as he ducked unnecessarily from Tog's dangling claws.

Tog swooped overhead to light the other side of the circle. The sopping stacks lit instantly from the heat of his blaze. The men cheered as Tog flew opposing circles around the group. The wraith would not easily escape now.

Rika nodded to Anna as Tog lit another spot in the dwindling circle of fire. "I believe so," he told the men. "Perhaps dragons help each other more than anyone knows."

With their attention on Tog, the wraith struggled through the circle, pulling at its tether and trying to avoid the dragon fires. A few men kept it away from them, but one of the men slipped in the mud. Instead of attacking the man, the wraith slipped through the incomplete cage. It swung around another man and dodged two more, finally sweeping behind Jarek to catch Anna unawares. With two hands beside her head, it lifted her into the air.

Hiro roared as wisps issued from Anna from the wraith's deadly effort. Without thinking Hiro wrapped his tail around Anna's waist and pivoted in the air to yank her free of its grip. He flung her to the ground and she slid in the mud across the circle from the monster. Jarek and Rika dove out of the way. Hiro attacked the wraith with fire and claw. When they had no effect, he lifted himself back into the air and away from it.

"We can't kill it without the ribbon! Can we?" Ammik yelled.

"We have to keep trying!" Rika called back.

Hiro dove at the beast with a roar. Back-drafting his wings just hard enough, he tried to claw the monster, but swept through it as easily as Ammik's axes. The wraith ignored his attempts and moved past the black dragon toward Jarek, he being the closest human bait.

One of the other men tried to use a burning log to steer the wraith from Jarek, but the pouring rain doused the minute flame. Both men and a few others fell to the ground as Hiro dove down at the wraith again with a burst of flame to announce himself. The wraith in turn swept to the side as Hiro tried to hedge it with fire. But he knew he couldn't keep this up forever.

He corralled the creature with flame until it finally turned its dark head toward Hiro. Still back-drafting, he opened his mouth to flood the wraith in flame, but the fire in his belly guttered. The wraith's hands stood out on either side of Hiro's snout. They had to reach much wider than around the sides of the humans' heads, but were apparently effective enough to control a fully grown dragon. He felt his legs slam against the ground.

Gagging, Hiro tried to force fire into his mouth. Something, anything, to spit at the creature. Hiro could feel warmth that should have allowed him to control his body being drawn out through his nose. His tail went cold. Lifeless. Then his hind legs. He felt the draw of heat go out from him again. His wings shivered. He realized this pitiful black creature might end his life here and now.

Cold crept up his spine when suddenly he saw a human head appear between himself and the wraith. Warmth flowed back in and pushed the cold away from Hiro's lungs and belly. He recognized Rika's head in the wraith's grasp. Warmth spread, banishing cold from his wings. The wraith took one draft from Rika. Fire burned hotter than it ever had in Hiro's heart. The wraith tossed Rika's lifeless body to the mud.

Flame washed over Hiro from behind to cover the wraith in front of him before it could reach its arms to Hiro again. Hiro's head sank to the ground. Tog roared and loosed more fire. But Hiro could only see the cold, empty, mud-splattered eyes of the human man on the ground, Rika.

Tog stood over him with relentless fire on the monster. Hiro shook his head. Rika. Dead. He became aware of Anna screaming and pushing past Tog. Jarek stood behind her, waving his arms at the wraith. Hiro pushed himself from the ground and shook his head again. Several other men had dropped their dragon-fired logs and waved their arms to distract the creature. Why would they do that?

Seeing his friend's strength return, Tog jumped into the air again. He didn't use his flame to protect the men, but concentrated on re-lighting the logs in the circle.

Rika had sacrificed himself. Hiro stood to his full height in front of the wraith. When its head swiveled back to him, he drowned it again in fire. Again and again he tried, hoping the fire would eventually take some effect on the creature despite the loss of the ribbon.

Finally, the wraith sank to the ground to avoid another burst of Hiro's flame, but immediately came back up with Jarek's head between its black fists. Hiro growled, baring his fangs. With his boots a claw length out of the mud, Jarek lashed out with his feet and hands. All of them passed through the shadowy creature, until his left hand slipped into the wraith's cowl where a face should have been. The wraith howled.

Jarek's eyes widened a moment before he howled, too. Hiro watched in shock as both creatures bellowed in pain. While the wraith's head whipped from side to side, Jarek forced his eyes to Hiro. "Fire!" he screamed. When Hiro hesitated, Jarek looked back at the wraith. With his hand shoved deep in the creature's cowl, he shook with fury. "HIRO, FIRE! NOW! FIRE!"

Laying his tongue to the side, he roared flame. With the precision of a butcher's knife, Hiro's fire sliced between Jarek and the wraith, to envelope the monster but protect the human. He almost stopped as human and wraith alike continued to screech and thrash in pain. He started to close his mouth as the other humans, Anna included, yelled for

Hiro to stop. But when he noticed a snake of smoke rising from the wraith, he ran closer to the pair and seared the wraith with even hotter flame.

Finally, Jarek dropped to the ground. Amidst his moans, Hiro watched as the wraith shriveled into a steaming mass and sank into the ground. Smoke issued for a moment before the black streak on the ground, largely unnoticed by the humans, fled across the sodden ground into the forest of the mountains beyond. Hiro closed his eyes for a moment, hoping Prak had his own job well in claw, and turned back to inspect Jarek.

Anna hovered over the human, whispering comforting words to him. Most of the men sagged on their feet or sat in the mud. A few had retrieved weapons and eyed Hiro.

"What happened?" Ammik yelled.

"Is it dead?" another man asked. Someone else stood over Rika's body.

"I believe so," Anna said. She turned away from Jarek to glare into Hiro's eyes.

"What did he do to Jarek?" Ammik yelled. He faced Hiro gripping his axes.

Jarek, regaining control, struggled upright but couldn't quite get to his feet. His right arm cradled his left. "He did what I asked him to."

"He could've killed you," Ammik yelled again. One axe drew back in a strong arm.

"It had to be done," Jarek growled. His tone reminded Hiro of Rakgar.

Tog landed a few dragon lengths away. Hiro knew that if the humans turned on him now they could both fly away easily. He kept his focus on Ammik.

"The ribbon," Jarek continued, as Anna helped him to his feet, "was made of human skin." He draped his right arm around her shoulder, exposing the charred stump of a hand on his left.

"Human—?" Anna stared into Jarek's face for a moment, then clutched the front of her shirt as she squeezed her eyes shut. Finally opening them again, she whispered, "I knew it felt familiar."

Ammik's axes finally fell. "What do we do about these dragons?"

"They'll do you no harm." Anna looked up at Hiro. "Thank you," she whispered. Then louder she exclaimed, "Home!" She jerked her head toward Tog.

Hiro only pretended to hesitate before slinking around the circle of men to crawl out of the smoldering ring to where Tog waited. Without waiting for a question, Tog placed his nose in front of Hiro's to blow a memory into his face.

Instantly Hiro was in a strange cave; he thought it must have been Surneen's because she sat posed in front of him with her head held high. "You don't understand," Tog's voice issued from Hiro's point of view, "what Hiro's doing is against dragon law. I can't be part of it."

Surneen nodded. "But it's also very dangerous, yes?"

"Extremely."

"And you can't tell me what he's doing?"

"I've given my wyrd."

"*Well*," *Surneen curled on the ground but displayed the gray faceted heart in one claw, "I won't use this to make you tell me, but I would think you a coward if you're not willing to help a friend in danger.*"

"*You think I should—*"

"*Don't worry,*" *she said over him, "I'll be here when you return.*"

Hiro blinked back into the pouring rain around him as Tog backed away. Not waiting for a signal, Tog turned and leapt into the sky. Hiro watched for a moment as another man came to lift Jarek from Anna's shoulder. Eight of the men lifted Rika's body from next to the fire, placed it on their shoulders and trudged through the mud with their heads down. Hiro wondered if their stooped posture might not have been from the rain. These humans certainly were different.

32

AWAITING A MEMORY

"Has Prak returned?" Hiro yelled, galloping into Rakgar's lair. A couple of dans from The Watch followed him and three little fledglings squealed as a dan taught them to fly in one of the wide, attached caverns.

"Hiro?" Rakgar waved away Milah and Mitashio, who grimaced at Hiro for the interruption. "I thought he stayed with you."

"He—" Hiro's voice caught when he saw Prak's mother, Fahrynak, follow Tog into the cavern. "I asked him to find whoever had conjured the creature, but I thought he would return before me." He hesitated to meet the large blue dame's worried eyes.

"He hasn't made it back yet," Tog said from Fahrynak's side. Tog and Hiro had separated upon entering the Rock Clouds. If Tog had found Prak he would have told Hiro to go back to his own cave where the smaller dragon would be.

Hiro's eyes drew back to Fahrynak as she stood staring at him from a side wall. "We searched for him on the way. We doubled back several times. All he needed to do was look for whoever—I didn't want him in any—" He finally ceased babbling with a sigh.

Rakgar's gaze finally left Hiro. He tilted his head to Milah, Mitashio and the others. "Would you please leave us a moment? Tog," he gestured to Prak's mother, "please accompany Fahrynak outside to await her son."

Once the lair cleared, Rakgar rounded on Hiro. "What did you do?"

Hiro rolled his shoulder. "We killed the wraith. When we got there the humans had surrounded it using farm tools. It had already killed one human and grabbed another. We flew over and I burned the wraith and the human." He tried not to flinch at the thought of Jarek's screams and Rika's glassy eyes. But far from being relieved, Rakgar narrowed his eyes. Hiro searched for a change in subject before he could request Hiro's memories. "Has Priya returned?"

Rakgar growled again and shook his head. Hiro had only a moment to register the anger in that growl before hearing the call outside. Prak had arrived.

"Prak!" Hiro yelled when the little brown dragon sidled into Rakgar's lair. "Where have you been? We've been worried!"

He met Prak and Tog near the entrance as Fahrynak, Milah, Mitashio, the others and more, followed them hesitantly into the lair. With a nod from Rakgar, they continued past the trio to their previous places.

Prak's usual chatter unnerved Hiro by its absence as the little dragon tromped in from the rain with his head down. "I stopped to talk to the centaurs," he muttered. "I felt I owed them an explanation."

Hiro dropped his voice. "An explanation of what?"

Prak tilted his head at Hiro as he waited until the other dragons were out of hearing. "Who really conjured the wraith."

"Prak," Rakgar's bellow bounced off the stone walls to reach them, "come here!"

Without acknowledging Rakgar's command, Prak reached his nose toward Hiro.

"Prak!" Rakgar called again, pushing past the other dragons. "Come here now. We need to contain all information. Give only myself your memories."

Prak continued the motion toward Hiro.

"Did you hear your Rakgar?" Mitashio called from beside the leader. "Do as you're told, young one!"

Prak dipped his head for a moment. He narrowed his eyes at Rakgar and whispered, "Will you order me like a human king?"

Silence.

Prak lifted his head to meet Hiro's nose. In a flash, Hiro saw the memory through Prak's keen night vision. *The wraith shadow stretching over the muddy ground next to his hiding place. The distant glow of fire, but no distinct shapes. Hiro watched through Prak's eyes as the snake-like shadow fled like a taut string pulled too far. When it ricocheted, he heard a grunt and some underbrush beyond him rustled.*

The brush shifted more as someone stood on weak legs from behind it. Prak's vision caught pointed ears drooping from exhaustion, transparent skin that couldn't hide the rage in its eyes and white-and-black-streaked hair in matted clumps. Before Prak could move, its wings spread to carry the unnamed faerie away.

Hiro blinked at Prak as Rakgar growled. "How dare you disobey me?"

But Prak faced Rakgar with courage Hiro had not credited him for having. "I gave Hiro my wyrd, Rakgar. Would you have me break it?" Then he breathed the memory to Rakgar.

Hiro didn't move. He barely took a breath until his leader blinked away the same memory Prak had given him.

"Now you see for yourself," Hiro whispered. "The faeries cannot be trusted." He gazed up at Rakgar. "And I no longer believe the humans are as evil as I once believed."

"Have you returned your mind?" Milah growled.

"The faeries are our allies, Hiro," Rakgar said over the mutters around them. "They always have been."

"I won't trust the faeries any longer," Hiro growled back, "and I don't think you should either."

"Will you trust a human?" Rakgar's eye held knowing.

"I don't know," Hiro hemmed. "Perhaps there could be worse things."

Hiro turned to leave the curses behind him, but Rakgar called to him again. "Will you no longer teach the hatchlings, then? You were doing so well with their training."

"No," he said over his shoulder, "I believe I would prefer to be on Priya's contingent again."

Rakgar nodded and Hiro started to leave again with Prak following close behind. "Be wary, Hiro." The tone of Rakgar's voice made Hiro spin around, expecting an attack, but Rakgar only watched him. "Everything you see on the surface is a lie. Humans are bred from deceit. You can't trust anything you see or hear on the surface."

"Like Shampy's lie about who conjured the wraith?"

"You can't mistrust all on the actions of the few. Just as you can't *trust* all on the actions of the few."

A thought sprang to Hiro's mind as if someone had given him a memory. He remembered his father dying on a frozen forest floor. "There is a reason to every word. A purpose to every action," he had said.

"I will think on it, Rakgar." Hiro bowed his head before leaving with his Prak-sized shadow.

33

JUST EXISTENCE

"Qialla," Philip inclined his head to the faerie gliding through the audience hall doors. Kradik, Philip knew, was overseeing preparations for their research venture to the Great Northern Mountain. "It's been more than seven days since the dragon sighting in the Torthoth Mountains. I would think the dragon would have attacked by now." He tried to keep his foot from tapping. These past few days, he'd been on edge about everything, waiting for an attack that Anna insisted wouldn't come.

Qialla nodded the dark cowl of his cloak. "It seems the attack has been prevented somehow. I searched my crystal ball only this hour and found that the dragon has returned to the Rock Clouds." He shrugged, "Perhaps it will seek vengeance another day."

Anna had been right. She had come back to the castle the morning after their words together (apparently, gone to stop the beast herself!) and sworn to Philip that the attack wouldn't come. As if she and a handful of villagers could manage what the King's Guard could not. In fact, she swore it wasn't a dragon attacking at all, but something called an "Earth Wraith." Philip realized he was chewing the inside of his lip and twitched it away from his teeth. The movement must have seemed like impatience to Qialla.

"Never fear, Your Majesty," he said, "the dragon will be dealt swift justice for previous attacks. Kradik and I will leave tomorrow and by spring you'll have a weapon more powerful than any dragon. And ten times more deadly."

———

Safe in his lair, Hiro curled on the floor, not really seeing the two other dragons watching him. "What do we do now, Hiro?" Prak asked.

Hiro sighed. "Nothing," he answered. "We live our lives. We complete our assignments. We care for the young and do as we're told."

"But the faeries—" Prak tried again.

"The faeries aren't here." Hiro thumped his head on his claws. "And I intend to live my life as if they don't exist."

"And the humans?" Tog said, scratching at the ground. "Do they exist?"

"They exist." Twisting his neck so they couldn't see the uncertainty in his eyes, Hiro said, "I intend to watch them with both eyes and all four claws."

THE END

The adventure continues in…

THE HEART OF

AVONOA

Avonoa Series Book Three!!

Note to Readers!

I hope you are enjoying the adventure in Avonoa as much
as I enjoyed creating it! Although I love to write and
create these stories, being an independent author is hard.
I don't have teams of people ghost-writing, editing,
formatting and marketing for me. I do it all on my own,
so my only support comes from readers like you! Thank
you for supporting me and my craft.

Another way you can support a lowly indie author like
myself is to leave me a review. Feel free to use the link
above to let others know how much you enjoyed the
story and you can pick up the next book at the same time!
Enjoy the adventure!!

You can also sign up for my newsletter to be the first to
hear about sales, signing events and new books! Sign up
at avonoa.com, hrbcollotzi.com, or
peopleofthestorm.com.

Or follow me on social media…
Facebook @hrbcollotzi
Instagram @hrbcolloti

THE HEART OF

AVONOA

Every Heart Breaks!

"Protect your heart!" Hiro's father and every other dan in the dragon ruck grew up hearing these words from their mentors. When your heart breaks for a dame, she can control you…or ruin you.

Control. Power. These are things not taken lightly. So why is it that Hiro's heart is so easily swayed? But not toward the one he prefers.

With an enemy army on the horizon and the possible discovery of a dragon poison, why should he worry about his heart breaking?